FURTHER TALES OF
LITTLE GREY RABBIT

FURTHER TALES OF LITTLE GREY RABBIT

by Denis Judd
after Alison Uttley

Pictures by
Margaret Tempest

COLLINS

William Collins Sons & Co Ltd
London · Glasgow · Sydney · Auckland
Toronto · Johannesburg

First published 1989
© text The Alison Uttley Literary Property Trust
and Denis Judd 1989

© illustrations The Estate of Margaret Tempest 1989

A CIP catalogue record for this book
is available from the British Library.

ISBN 0 00 194201-8

Printed and bound in Spain by
GRUPO NERECAN - TONSA, San Sebastian

Contents

*The author and publishers wish to thank
Mrs Joyce Gray who is the owner of the
original illustrations in this book.*

THE STORY BEHIND
THIS BOOK

A few years ago, Collins acquired over sixty pre-viously unpublished Margaret Tempest pictures of the various characters depicted in the greatly loved and best selling tales of Little Grey Rabbit.

At just this time, I had been invited by Mrs Uttley's literary trustees to write the authorized biography. I was deeply immersed in my researches, which included the careful reading of nearly forty volumes of Alison's candid, detailed and very illuminating diaries.

When my editor at Collins, Susan Dickinson, asked me to write some new stories around the Tempest pictures I felt joy, and disquiet – for what would Mrs Uttley have thought? I was comforted by the idea that Alison would certainly *not* have wanted Margaret Tempest's pictures to have appeared without some appropriate accompanying words. I have tried, as the stories unfolded, to be as faithful as possible to Mrs Uttley's strongly individualistic style, and to maintain the integrity of the richly varied characters she created – Fuzzypeg, Water-at, Hare, Moldy Warp, Wise Owl and the rest. I have also attempted, as Alison did (though conscious of today's context) to "take the children into a land without fear – although there are small fears which are surmounted."

Above all, I have written these further tales as a warm and deeply felt tribute to Alison Uttley's literary skills and to the imaginative world she invented. If those who read these new stories get half as much pleasure in the process as I have from writing them, I shall be overjoyed.

Denis Judd

(Author of *Alison Uttley:* The Life of a Country Child,
and a Trustee of Alison Uttley's Literary Property)

Fuzzypeg
Gets a Surprise

Very early one morning, there was a 'Rat-a-Tat' at the door of Mr and Mrs Hedgehog's house. Mrs Hedgehog was cooking breakfast, while little Fuzzypeg was upstairs splashing water from his washing basin over his prickly head.

"See who that is, Fuzzypeg, my dear," called Mrs Hedgehog as she put another egg into the frying pan.

Fuzzypeg pulled his newly-mended school smock over his head and bounced downstairs like a spiky ball.

He opened the kitchen door, and blinked in the sunlight. "Mother!" he called. "It's Postman Robin. He's got a letter for us."

Mrs Hedgehog sighed, and pushed the pan to one side. Wiping her hands on her white apron, she came to the door and stood beside her son.

"Good morning, Postman," said she.

"Morning, ma'am," replied Robin cheerfully. He plucked a leafy letter from his postbag and held it out for Mrs Hedgehog to take. Then he tilted his head to one side and watched curiously.

Mrs Hedgehog opened the little green letter and turned it over in her hand. "Bless me," she said softly, as she peered at the words scratched upon its shiny surface.

"What does it say, Mother? What does it say?" cried Fuzzypeg, standing on tip-toes to see the letter.

11

"It says . . ." replied Mrs Hedgehog, uncertainly. Then she paused, frowning. "It says that . . . why, here's your father coming up the path, Fuzzypeg, bringing the milk for breakfast!"

"Any reply, ma'am?" asked Robin. He was anxious to be off, for as well as the letters in his bag, he had a telegram to deliver to Wise Owl.

Mrs Hedgehog pushed the green letter into the pocket of her apron. "No thank you, Postman," she said firmly.

As Robin flew off, Milkman Hedgehog set down his wooden pails on the doorstep. The creamy milk was warm and frothy, and soon Mrs Hedgehog was bustling about setting the food and drink on the breakfast table.

As soon as the three of them were seated, Fuzzypeg burst out in his excited squeak, "Oh, Father, there's a letter. Postman Robin brought it. What does it say? Mother won't tell me. What's in it? I have to go to school soon, and I want to know. Please, Father!"

Old Hedgehog lifted his head from his mug of milk. "Hold hard, Fuzzypeg. Don't be in such a harum-scarum hurry."

He reached out his hand for the letter, which his wife had taken from her apron pocket.

First he held it at arm's length. Then he placed it on the table and took a bite of his fried egg. After wiping his mouth on the corner of his neckerchief, he next held the letter very close to his eyes. Finally he set it down again and sighed.

"This here letter's got me all moithered," said he. "I'm no scollard, not I. Your mother, and you, Fuzzypeg, have got a sight more larning than I." He passed the letter back to his wife.

"But what does the letter say?" asked Fuzzypeg. He felt as if he would burst into tears at any moment.

His mother looked up from the letter and smiled. "It says you will get a surprise, Fuzzypeg," she said kindly. "A surprise soon, very soon."

"A surprise!" cried Fuzzypeg. But before he could find out what the surprise might be, it was time for school. His mother put his satchel over his shoulder and popped his sandwiches inside its big pocket.

"Don't forget your quill pen, my boy!" Old Hedgehog called after his son as he ran down the path. "And mind your Ps and Qs!"

"Bother my Ps and Qs" muttered Fuzzypeg as he set off. "What about my surprise?"

Soon he was at the cottage of his cousins, Bill and Tim Hedgehog, who lived in the nearby larch wood.

Their mother was getting them ready for school, brushing Tim's spiky hair while Bill knelt down to do up his shoelaces.

"I'm going to have a surprise, I am," said Fuzzypeg, importantly, as he stood in the doorway.

Bill jumped up, a shoelace still undone. "A surprise – what is it, a present?" he asked. "Perhaps it's a

golden egg," called Tim, wriggling away from his mother's brushing. "Or a unicorn!"

"Be off with you," said the twins' mother, bundling them out of doors and smiling to herself as the three little figures trotted down the lane.

They began to cross the common, discussing in their high-pitched voices what Fuzzypeg's surprise might be. Tim still fancied it would be a shining white unicorn, tossing its snowy mane and pawing the ground with its slender hoof, magical and mysterious. Bill, though, began to doubt whether there was going to be a surprise at all.

The sun was now beating down as they trudged across the common. Honey bees flew between the purple clumps of heather, and a skylark fluttered, singing, high above their heads.

Fuzzypeg was growing hot and cross. For two pins he would have pushed Bill into a gorse bush, but remembered that his cousin was just as prickly as the bush, and thought better of it.

Soon the three cousins began to argue, and then to fight in a struggling, spiny bundle that rolled down a gentle slope near the edge of the common.

As they untangled themselves, and stood up, shaking the grass from their spikes, they saw, a short way off, a strange sight.

Near a little tent made out of a piece of old sailcloth stood a gypsy rabbit with a red shawl over her shoulders, wearing a bright yellow headscarf. She was stirring a black cooking pot over a blazing fire of beech twigs. On the grass was a knife, and a wooden basket containing newly-made clothes pegs.

As she stirred the pot, from which came a rich smell of carrots and turnips and strange-scented herbs, she sang softly to herself in a language from far away and long ago.

Fuzzypeg, Tim and Bill stared at her in wonderment, not daring to speak.

Suddenly, without looking up, she called out, "Come nearer, my dears. I won't harm you."

The three little hedgehogs clutched each others' hands and crept close to the fire.

15

The gypsy suddenly raised her head and looked at them. Her eyes were amber, and in them, Fuzzypeg thought he saw the images of strange creatures and wondrous places, dimly remembered.

"Can I help you, my dears?" she said, smiling. "You may share my breakfast. Or maybe I can tell your fortunes?"

Fuzzypeg shook his head. "We've had our breakfasts, missus," said he. "But . . ." and here he hesitated, and stared at his toes.

"Yes?" said the gypsy, gently.

"Fuzzypeg has got a surprise," suddenly squeaked Tim. "But he doesn't know what it is."

The gypsy rabbit nodded as if she had always known, and reaching into a purse hanging from her waist she took a pinch of powder and cast it into the fire.

The flames leapt and flickered, turning green and blue, making fantastical pictures amid the smoke.

As the fire crackled, she began to sing in a low, soft voice:

> "Riddle-me-ree, riddle-me-ree,
> Look in the fire and who can you see?
> One is older than your mother,
> But a mother all the same.
> One is older than your father,
> And he bears your father's name."

The gypsy beckoned Fuzzypeg and the twins to come closer to the fire.

"What do you see, my dears?" she whispered.

Fuzzypeg peered at the dancing flames. Suddenly he gave a shrill cry. "I see them! I can see it all."

"Hush!" said the gypsy, quickly laying her paw against Fuzzypeg's mouth. "It's your surprise. Say it aloud and it may not come true. Now, off you go, and remember, not a word!"

She turned back to the fire and began softly singing once more to herself.

Fuzzypeg scampered all the way to school, with the twins at his heels begging to know what he had seen in the fire.

He squeezed under the big gate and into Daisy Field, crossed the meadow studded with small, bright flowers like stars, and came at last, puffing and panting, to Jonathan Rabbit's school. Tim and Bill trailed behind, grumbling that they still did not know what their cousin's surprise might be.

All day at school Fuzzypeg was quietly happy, hugging his secret to himself, and not daring to speak too much in case it should somehow pop out and be lost. He daydreamed his way through the counting lesson, saying "one, two, shoe my buckle," and did not hear half the questions that Old Jonathan asked his pupils in their nature studies.

But he did hear the ringing of the harebells which told all the little animals that school was over for the day.

Fuzzypeg ran home as fast as he could, leaving Tim and Bill puffing and complaining behind him.

He threw open the door of his cottage, almost knocking his father over as he did so.

"What did they larn you today, my son, apart from running wild like a March hare?" asked Old Hedgehog, mildly.

"Are they? The surprise . . . is it?" gasped Fuzzypeg.

"What can he mean, Husband?" said Mrs Hedgehog, smiling at her son.

Just then, there was the sound of a stick tapping on

the path outside.

Fuzzypeg turned and dashed down the path uttering little squeaks of delight. From the doorway of their cottage Mr and Mrs Hedgehog beamed as their son flung himself into the arms of his grandparents.

"What a surprise, eh, Fuzzypeg?" Old Hedgehog called out.

Fuzzypeg, hugging first his grandmother, then his grandfather, thought suddenly of the dancing flames of the gypsy's fire and what he had seen there. But all he wanted to say was, "Oh yes, Father, the best surprise in the world."

Mrs Webster's Busy Day

Mrs Webster, Water-rat's housekeeper, knocked on his bedroom door very early one morning. It was only just light outside. The sun was still low in the sky, turning the wispy clouds in its path a soft pink, and the creatures of the riverbank were beginning to stir.

Water-rat opened his eyes at Mrs Webster's knock. "Come in!" he called. Then he pulled the blankets up to his chin and waited.

Mrs Webster waddled towards his bed, carrying a cup of hot chocolate on a tray.

"Time to get up, sir," said she as she handed Water-rat the steaming, sweet-smelling drink. She glanced at the port-hole above the bed. "Oh dear, you didn't close your window and draw your curtains, sir," she remarked disapprovingly.

"Fresh air, my dear Mrs Webster!" replied Water-rat, sitting up. "The bracing breezes from the salty sea, don't you know?"

"But we're nowhere near the sea here," grumbled Mrs Webster as she turned to go.

"That's just it," cried Water-rat. "That's why I wanted an early call. I'm going to the sea for the day, rowing down the river until I reach the briny ocean."

"I don't fancy any sort of ocean," Mrs Webster muttered as she closed the bedroom door. "Give me our river and fresh water any time."

Within an hour Water-rat had dressed, eaten a hearty breakfast and tossed the picnic hamper into the 'Saucy Nancy'.

Mrs Webster fussed round him. "Now, sir," she said. "Have you packed in your pocket handkerchief?"

"Yes, Mrs Webster," sighed Water-rat.

"And your fresh water jar? And the compass, sir, in case you lose your bearings?"

Water-rat nodded. "And when can we expect you back, sir?" the good housekeeper continued.

"Oh, in a day or two, I suppose," replied Water-rat airily. "Now I must get aboard. Goodbye, Mrs Webster. Try to have a little holiday while I'm gone. Get some rest."

With that, he stepped lightly into his boat and settled himself to the oars.

Mrs Webster waved as the 'Saucy Nancy' pulled away, heading downstream, and soon Water-rat was out of sight round a bend in the river.

" 'Get some rest!' " said Mrs Webster to herself as she turned back towards the house. " 'Have a little holiday!' That'll be the day. There's always work to

do if you're a housekeeper."

The first thing Mrs Webster did when she got back in the house was to clear up the breakfast table and wash the cups and plates.

Then she began on the bedrooms. Since Water-rat was going to be away for a while, she stripped his bed and hung the sheets outside to air in the fresh breeze. After that she went to her own bedroom.

Mrs Webster slept in a four-poster bed with pretty pink frills at the top and bottom. It was a good, solid, old bed that had been in Water-rat's family for years.

No doubt if he had ever got married he and his wife would have slept in it, like his mother and father before him. But Water-rat was a bachelor, and preferred the narrow sleeping berth under the port-hole.

"What a comfortable bed I've got," thought Mrs Webster as she changed the sheets and pillow-cases. "I can really get a good night's sleep after a hard day's work."

Carrying the sheets and pillow-cases and some other laundry in a big bundle, she made her way to the reeds at the river's edge.

"More washing, Mrs Webster?" asked the little brown Water-hen who was the laundress.

"Yes; it never ends," replied Mrs Webster as she put down the bundle. "Now mind you get Mr Water-rat's frilly shirts nice and clean."

"Ah, he's very particular over his frilly shirts, ain't he?" remarked the Water-hen. "Very particular indeed. Still, it's a good drying day. I always says 'There's nothing like a good drying day', that's what I always says. What do you say, Mrs Webster?"

But Mrs Webster was already making her way back to the house thinking about her next task.

"A good spring-cleaning, that's what's needed," said she as she closed the front door behind her.

For the rest of the morning Mrs Webster dusted and polished. She hung the rugs outside and beat them with a bamboo cane. Then she got a pail of water and some soap and scrubbed the floors and all the narrow passages in the house. She took down the curtains and shook them in the fresh air.

After a late, and quickly taken lunch, Mrs Webster made a dozen jars of lily-bud jam and some mint jellies.

Putting a few of the jars, which were still warm, into her basket, she locked the front door and went off visiting.

The first house she called at belonged to a family of field mice. There were eleven young mice in the family and Mrs Webster often went to play with them and to lend their mother a hand.

When Mrs Webster stepped into the crowded kitchen she was greeted with squeaks of delight. There seemed to be young mice everywhere – playing on the floor,

25

reading by the fire, toasting bread or just scampering about. Two of the youngest were sitting on their father's knee, while another was standing on tip-toes to watch her mother iron.

Soon Mrs Webster was on her hands and knees helping to build a tower of wooden bricks. Then she made the mother mouse sit by the fire while she finished off the ironing. More bread was toasted, and the little mice were given three jars of lily-bud jam to spread on it.

By the time tea was over, the room was full of happy, sticky little mice, and two of the jam jars were empty.

As Mrs Webster was walking home, feeling tired but happy, Rat suddenly stepped out from the hedgerow and stood in her path.

Mrs Webster gasped and clutched her basket more tightly than before.

Rat touched his cap. "Evening, Mrs Webster, ma'am," he said. "I needs your help, if you'll be so kind, and seeing as how we're both rats, like."

"Well!" replied Mrs Webster indignantly. " 'Both rats', indeed! I'll have you know that we water-rats are quite different from your sort of rat. We aren't nasty, thieving creatures, skulking in the shadows."

She started to walk on. "Oh, please, missus," cried Rat. "Don't leave so hasty! There's sickness at home. Me wife and the little'un and the wife's sister, they're all took ill."

Mrs Webster peered at him. Never had she seen Rat look so miserable.

A little later, Rat showed Mrs Webster into the room where the sick animals lay huddled under their blankets. Even though the evening was a warm one, they were shivering and complaining of the cold.

"Stick out your tongues!" said Mrs Webster briskly. She peeped down their throats, and put her paw on their hot foreheads.

"They've got a fever," she announced. "Your

house is too draughty and damp, Rat. Why don't you mend the windows?"

Rat opened his mouth to reply, but Mrs Webster cut him short.

"Off you go," said she. "Bring me some elder-flower from the hedgerows, and some wild herbs from the meadows."

Rat was back in half an hour, his pockets stuffed with white elderflower and the grey-green herbs.

Mrs Webster made a big pot of elderflower tea, which the sick animals drank eagerly. Then she poured boiling water over the herbs and made each of them inhale the sharp, spicy steam. Soon all three were sound asleep, breathing easily.

It was dark by the time Mrs Webster got home. Water-rat had not yet returned, but she laid out some cold food on the kitchen table in case he should arrive after she had gone to sleep and feel hungry from his travels. Only then did she climb into her comfortable four-poster bed and fall at once into a deep sleep.

Water-rat arrived home after breakfast on the next morning. He looked travel-stained and weary, and, much to Mrs Webster's surprise, was standing in a blue punt which he pushed along with a pole.

"Where's the 'Saucy Nancy', sir?" asked Mrs Webster anxiously. Water-rat tied up the punt and climbed slowly onto the jetty.

"Oh, Mrs Webster," he groaned. "What a busy

time I've had. I never got to the sea. Why, I couldn't even smell the salty breezes, or hear the sea-gulls. It was those tiresome white ducks. They surrounded the boat and started diving and pushing and trying to snatch the picnic basket."

"Did they steal the watercress sandwiches?" asked Mrs Webster.

"No, much worse than that," replied Water-rat. "They hustled and bustled round me so much that I dropped an oar and the 'Saucy Nancy' ran aground in the shallows and started to leak."

"Where's the boat now, sir?" Mrs Webster enquired as Water-rat stumbled into the house and flopped down on a chair.

"I managed to paddle her back upstream," answered Water-rat, "to Otter's house. It was dark when I arrived. He promised to mend the leak, and he lent me the punt to come home as soon as it was light. Oh, Mrs Webster! What a busy day I've had."

"Yes, indeed, sir," replied Mrs Webster.

"And you, Mrs Webster. Have you been taking it easy while I was away? A little holiday, eh?"

"Well, not exactly, sir," began Mrs Webster, but Water-rat just nodded.

"Good. Good," he said, absent-mindedly.

"All he ever thinks about is that dratted boat," muttered Mrs Webster, and she went into the kitchen and slammed the door.

A Narrow Escape

One warm, sunny morning Fuzzypeg's cousins, Tim and Bill, overslept.

They only woke up when their mother rushed into their bedroom. "Up you get, you sleepyheads!" she cried. "You'll be late for school."

As the twins sat up in bed, grumbling and rubbing their eyes, their mother pulled open the curtains and the pale yellow sunlight flooded into the room.

"What time is it, Mother?" asked Tim, yawning. "Time to be up," replied Mrs Hedgehog. "I was talking to Postman Robin, and he was telling me this and that, and I clean forgot the time."

· "I wish you had forgotten for a bit longer," complained Bill as he struggled out of bed.

"Come on, boys," cried their mother. "Get dressed and washed. Your breakfast's ready downstairs," and she began following them around, brushing their spikes and flapping her apron.

Soon the twins were sitting at the kitchen table eating their bread and milk, while Mrs Hedgehog bustled about making their sandwiches.

"I'm sure I've never been in such a pickle," said she. "I had the jam pot out only a moment ago, but I can't think what I've done with it."

Then Bill discovered that he had only got on one shoe.

"One-two, you can't buckle your shoe," sang Tim, who had both shoes on his feet.

"You've got my shoe!" said Bill, crossly. "Give it here."

But Tim danced round the room, mocking his twin brother, until Bill leaped at him in a rage and knocked him over.

"Oh, deary me!" sighed Mrs Hedgehog as she bent down to untangle the spiky, squeaking ball as it rolled over the kitchen floor.

In the end, Bill's missing shoe was discovered behind the grandfather clock, though how it got there nobody could say. Tim thought that a leprechaun might have hidden it away for a prank. But Bill thought it more likely that it was Tim's doing, and prepared once more to do battle with his brother.

Wearily, Mrs Hedgehog separated her struggling sons and packed them off to school.

As the twins ran down the path they turned and

waved to their mother standing at the front door.

"If you run all the way you won't be late," she called after them, but the wind caught her words and carried them high above the little hedgehogs and away among the trees of the larch wood.

After a while, the twins were out of breath and feeling hot and sweaty. Bill had got a pebble lodged inside his shoe, and Tim was complaining that he felt dizzy.

They sat down on a grassy bank, amid bindweed, cow parsley and forget-me-nots.

"I'm famished," said Tim. He took out his packet of sandwiches and began to eat them.

"They're your elevenses," protested Bill. But Tim

took no notice, and soon Bill had opened his own packet and eaten half the contents.

Feeling refreshed, the twins set off for school. The sun was climbing higher in the sky, and the butterflies were fluttering among the wild flowers.

They squeezed under the gate to the Daisy Field and saw their uncle, Milkman Hedgehog, walking towards them carrying his empty pails.

"Bless me!" cried Old Hedgehog as they met. "You boys must be playing truant. My little Fuzzypeg has been at school a good hour. Off with you! You'll never learn as much as Fuzzypeg if you play truant."

"What's playing truant?" muttered Tim, as the twins set off across the meadow at a steady trot.

"I specks it's a game like blind man's buff," replied Bill.

"Or snakes and ladders," suggested Tim.

"Or hunt the thimble," said Bill, beginning to gasp for breath.

A few minutes later they arrived, panting, at their school.

They knocked with the brass knocker and opened the little green door. As they walked into the schoolroom, many pairs of eyes were turned in their direction and some of the small animals began whispering to each other.

"Silence!" cried Old Jonathan Rabbit, rapping the stone that served as his desk with a ruler.

He picked up a dandelion clock and puffed at it.

" 'A diller, a dollar,
A ten-o'clock scholar,' "
said he. "You're late again, twins. You will have to stay in when the other pupils go out to eat their elevenses."

Bill nudged Tim who blurted out, "We've already eaten our elevenses, sir!"

"Then no wonder you are so late," replied Old Jonathan, gravely. "Don't do it again. Sit down and open your books."

The rest of the school day passed by peacefully and pleasantly. Old Jonathan told his pupils tales of long ago, of the beginning of the world and how dinosaurs and sabre-toothed tigers had once roamed over the countryside they each knew so well.

"I shouldn't like to meet one of those sabre-toothed tigers," whispered Bill to his cousin, Fuzzypeg. But Fuzzypeg muttered that it would be much worse to come face to face with Tyrannosaurus Rex, the flesh-eating dinosaur, and shuddered at the thought.

Then Water-rat arrived. He had moored his boat at the river bank and had walked over the meadow to show Old Jonathan's pupils some of his treasures. There was a glass case with a stuffed goldfish in it, and a pair of fine, silvery skates for winter sports. There were striped sea shells and a great white feather fallen from the wing of a swan.

The little animals crowded round Water-rat and listened wide-eyed as he told them of the minnows and sticklebacks that swam in the streams, and of the reeds that grew at the water's edge and which were dried and used for thatching their cottages.

At last it was time to go home.

Jonathan Rabbit called for silence. "Before school ends," he said, "I want to give you some advice."

He paused while one of the smallest field mice was put on somebody's lap in order to see better.

"Water-rat," said Jonathan, "has shown you interesting and beautiful things from the world you live in. I have told you of strange and dangerous creatures from long ago.

"But," and here he gazed sternly at two young rabbits who were beginning to giggle, "there are dangers nowadays as well. Be careful as you walk home. Do not talk to strangers, even though they may appear friendly. It is better to be safe than sorry."

At that, Jonathan nodded to the young hare who ran to shake the harebells for the end of school.

As Fuzzypeg, Bill and Tim walked home, taking the longer way over the common, they discussed what Old Jonathan had told them. Fuzzypeg thought that it was best to be careful, but Tim pooh-poohed the idea. "I likes talking to strangers," he said. "You gets to know them then. And sometimes they might give you something nice to eat."

They were still arguing when they stepped onto the edge of the common.

"Hush!" said Fuzzypeg. Tim fell silent, and Bill stopped in his tracks.

Several yards in front of them a group of animals stood round a wood fire. The father poked the fire to make it burn better, while the mother held a frying-pan, her small daughter standing at her side. Behind them a tent had been pitched, and another young member of the family was carrying a bundle of sticks towards the fire.

"Weasels," whispered Tim.

"But they've got black tips to their tails," protested Fuzzypeg. "They're not weasels. They're stoats, I reckons."

"What's stoats?" asked Bill.

"They're like weasels," replied Fuzzypeg quietly, "only bigger."

"And fiercer?" asked Bill, anxiously. "Like sabre-toothed tigers?"

"They're *not* stoats," said Tim, scornfully. "They're weasels. Anybody can see that. I bet you they aren't stoats, Fuzzypeg."

Tim and Fuzzypeg began to argue more loudly. Suddenly Tim said, "Right! I'm going to ask them what they are."

"Oh, no! Don't, Tim!" wailed Bill, but Tim was already on his way.

The largest of the strange animals lifted his head at Tim's approach. His wife turned to sniff the air, and their daughter gazed curiously at the little figure in his bright red smock.

Tim stopped in front of the fire.

"Please, sir," he began, in an undignified squeak. He was surprised to find that he was trembling.

"Yes, my dear?" replied the father animal softly.

"Is you stoats?" asked Tim, nervously. "Or weasels?"

"Stoats, my dear. Fancy not knowing that. You're a card you are, and no mistake!"

"Ain't he a card, my dears?" continued the stoat turning to his family with a wide smile.

He took a step closer to Tim and put his arm round his shoulders. "Come nearer the fire, my dear, and warm yourself."

"But I'm quite warm enough, thank you, sir,"

replied Tim, uncomfortably aware that the stoat had got him in a tight grip. "I'd best get back to my friends."

"Friends!" exclaimed the stoat. "Well, what an honour to be sure, eh, Wife?" He threw back his head and laughed, showing pointed yellow teeth. "Bring your friends over, and we'll have quite a feast in a little while.

"Wife!" he hissed out of the corner of his mouth. "Get some clay from the ditch yonder. Then we'll roll these young hedgehogs in it and bake 'em in the fire. Lovely, tasty food is baked hedgehog!

"Now, my dear," he said, bending over Tim with a gleam in his eye. But he got no further, for Tim, shocked by what he had overheard, bit him on the paw.

"Ow!" cried the stoat, letting go of Tim in his pain.

Crying with fright, Tim took to his heels and ran as fast as he could towards Fuzzypeg and Bill.

"Catch them!" shouted the stoat as he rubbed his paw.

"No, Husband!" said his wife firmly, standing in his way. "Horrible prickly things is hedgehogs. Let them go, I says."

"Let them go?" gasped the stoat. "Why, when they're baked proper, and you break off the clay, they're as good to eat as rabbit or chicken."

"Let them go, Husband," replied his wife. "We've got enough for supper as it is, and the children are

41

hungry." Grumbling, the stoat returned to poking the fire, cursing his bad luck.

The little hedgehogs arrived at Bill and Tim's cottage in a terrible state, short of breath and still scared out of their wits.

The twins' mother was shaking the table-cloth onto the lawn as they ran towards her.

"Why, whatever is it?" she cried. "You look as if you've seen a ghost."

"Oh, Mother," sobbed Tim. "It was worse than that. There were stoats. And they wanted to bake us and eat us!" He buried his face in his paws.

"Stoats!" said Mrs Hedgehog. "They're nearly as dangerous as foxes are stoats."

She took Tim's paws in hers. "Have you been poking your nose into other people's business again, Tim Hedgehog? You should know better."

Then she led the tearful little hedgehogs inside, where she gave them tea and mended their torn smocks.

News of the stoats' encampment soon spread, and that night Wise Owl swooped low over the common ready to drive them away. But there was no sign of them. The tent had gone, and all that remained were the ashes of the fire still glowing in the dark.

As for Tim, he now knows the difference between a weasel and a stoat. But more important still, he knows how dangerous it can be to speak to strangers.

Rat
Resists Temptation

It was winter and the Rat family were feeling the cold. Some days they stayed in bed until after midday, the mother and father huddled in their double bed, and the young rat tucked up in his basket on the floor. Even so, the winter wind reached through the broken window panes of their bedroom and nipped their noses with its frosty fingers.

The trouble was that Rat could find no work. He no longer had the awkward, troublesome knot in his tail that Squirrel had once tied, and it is true that his neighbours now thought better of him, but times were still hard. Once the harvest had been gathered in, and the farmyards and gardens had been tidied up for the winter, there were no more odd jobs for him to do.

Although Mrs Rat did her best to save food, and to use up all the kitchen scraps, it never seemed enough. The young rat was growing fast and was always hungry. So, as the weather grew steadily worse, the Rat family slept late and therefore didn't have to worry about breakfast. Sometimes they did without lunch as well.

But on this particular day the young rat woke up in the middle of the morning and began to cry.

Mrs Rat sat up in bed. She reached down to the basket and found the little white toy that Rat had carved out of a bone.

"There, there!" said she. "Play with your toy, little one." But the young rat whimpered, "I's hungry. I's cold."

Mrs Rat dug her husband in his ribs with her elbow. "Wake up, Rat!" she cried. "Our little one wants food. Go out and find some."

But Rat just groaned and pulled the blankets over his ears. The young rat now began to cry in earnest.

Angrily Mrs Rat shook her husband awake. "Get up, Rat! Off you go and find some work, you good-for-nothing creature!"

Cursing under his breath, Rat struggled out of bed. "Ooh! It's freezing, Wife!" he complained as he stood on the bare boards of the bedroom floor.

"Then you should have mended the broken window and fixed the shutter like I asked you to," she replied.

As Rat stumbled towards the front door, pulling on his check coat, his wife called after him, "And don't you come back until you've got some food!"

Rat searched in the hedgerows as he walked along, but all he found was an old sock and an empty, rusty tin can. He had better luck when he came to the little group of hazel bushes at the corner of Hearthstone Pasture. By shaking their branches he managed to dislodge a few nuts that the squirrels had missed. Rat counted them slowly, "One, two, five, three." He shook his head. "Bother this counting," said he. So he ate two of the biggest nuts and put the rest in his pocket.

A little later Rat sidled up to the farmyard. Nobody was about, so he crept up the narrow ladder that led to the hen-house. There, lying in the straw of the nest, were two large, brown eggs.

Rat put out his paw to touch one. It was still warm. "The Speckledy Hen must have just laid it," he said to himself. He thought of the rich, yellow yolk inside the egg, and of how the baby rat would enjoy gobbling it up.

"Surely the Speckledy Hen wouldn't miss one egg?" he thought. "She can always lay another, and she's a kindly soul."

But then he remembered the knot he had once had in his tail. "Perhaps it will come back if I steal the egg," he muttered. He turned and climbed swiftly down the ladder and ran out of the farmyard.

He had just got home and was proudly laying the hazel nuts out on the kitchen table when his wife heard footsteps approaching. Down the path came her sister with her three children.

Rat and his family went out to greet them. "Come inside, sister," cried Mrs Rat. "We've got some soup, and some . . ." She hesitated.

"And some nuts," added Rat. "The little'uns will enjoy them. Come inside, and welcome."

The next day Rat was up early looking for work and food. But many of the animals had gone into hibernation and were sleeping the winter away, and some of the birds had flown south to escape the cold. Milkman Hedgehog kindly gave Rat half a pail of milk, but he spilled most of it on the way home.

The day after that was no better, and Rat began to feel desperate.

He was trudging home, his paws in his pockets and the collar of his coat turned up against the bitter wind, when he spied the ugly little house where the weasels lived. The shutters were up, and thick black smoke was pouring out of the chimney.

Rat crept up to the window and peeped through a crack in the shutters. Around a blazing fire were gathered five weasels. They were drinking out of tin mugs and toasting cheese on the fire.

Screwing up his eyes, Rat recognized three of them as the bad weasels who had once kept Grey Rabbit a

prisoner and stolen eggs from the Speckledy Hen.

Suddenly William Weasel banged his tin mug on the table.

"Pipe down, you lot!" he shouted. Slowly the hubbub died away, but not quickly enough for William who pounced on his sister Winnie and cuffed her about the ears.

MARGARET TEMPEST

"That's better," sneered William, as his sister grumbled and rubbed her head.

"Get on with it, William," said Winkie Weasel sullenly.

"About tomorrow," began William. "The plan is

this. Winnie will hide near Grey Rabbit's house and wait until Hare goes out. Then, after a bit, she'll rush in and say, 'Oh deary-me, that nice Mr Hare's gone and broke his leg.' "

"Or his neck?" suggested Winnie, but William raised his paw and she flinched and fell silent.

"Broke his leg," continued William. "Out Grey Rabbit will rush, sobbing away."

"Screaming, maybe," said Winkie, smiling broadly.

"Sobbing!" shouted William. "Sobbing, I says, and sobbing it is."

"Anyway," he went on, scowling at his brother, "Grey Rabbit and Squirrel, if she's there, will rush off to help Hare and then . . ."

"And then!" cried Winkie. "In we nips and pinches all the grub!"

"Loaves of bread! Pats of butter," chanted Winnie.

"Currant buns! New-laid eggs!" shouted the other weasels.

Outside the window, Rat licked his lips. What he'd give for some of that food! How the young rat would shriek with joy.

"Maybe I can tag along?" he thought. "Then I could get into Grey Rabbit's house after the weasels and pick up anything they've left."

Suddenly he was aware of a sharp pain in his tail, just where the knot had once been, and, turning away from the window, he slunk off deep in thought.

51

Hungry as he was, Rat decided not to join the weasels in their wicked plan. That evening he went to Grey Rabbit's house and told her everything.

"Really!" said Squirrel indignantly.

"Just let me get at those weasels!" cried Hare dancing round the kitchen. He opened the door and peeped outside. "Oh dear!" he said. "It's getting rather dark. I'd better wait until tomorrow." But Grey Rabbit just sat quietly, her eyes open wide.

Later that night Rat crept up to Wise Owl's beech tree and, timidly waving a white handkerchief for a truce, told him of the weasels' plot.

Wise Owl flew straightway to the weasels' house and shook the shutters. "Ho, you wretched weasels!" he hooted. "We know about your evil plans. If any of you are here at break of day I shall pull down the door and eat you up!"

So, as had happened before, the weasels had to pack up their belongings and move somewhere else until all the trouble had died down.

The next morning the young rat was standing with his parents outside his house pumping water into a bucket when Grey Rabbit walked down the path carrying her basket.

Rat quickly went to meet her. Soon she was sitting on the only good chair in the kitchen, with the young rat on her lap.

"I can't thank you enough, dear Rat, for warning

us of the danger we were in," said Grey Rabbit. She took the checked cloth from the top of the basket and let the young rat peep inside. Squeaking with delight, he took out all manner of good things to eat – cakes and pies and cheeses and a jar of wild honey.

"Oh, you shouldn't, ma'am," said Mrs Rat. "And we've got nothing in the house to give you. Not even a crust of bread." She began to cry.

"There, there," said Grey Rabbit softly. "I know that times have been hard for you."

"Wait," mumbled Rat. He went quickly outside and returned with a tumbler brimming with sparkling water. "From our pump over the spring," said he.

Grey Rabbit lifted the tumbler to the light. "How clear the water is!" she observed. "And look at the

little bubbles dancing to the surface."

She sipped. "I've never tasted better water in my life," she declared. "not even from the brook that runs past our house. This is water fit for a king."

"Or for a queen," squeaked the small rat smiling shyly up at her, and they all laughed.

After that, things got better for Rat and his family. He once more took to carving fine little toys and ornaments from bones, and, since Christmas was coming, there was a great demand for them as presents. When customers came to see her husband's handiwork, Mrs Rat would offer each of them a glass of spring water, remarking, "Miss Grey Rabbit says it's fit for a king."

Christmas Eve came at last, and with it snow, fluttering down from the grey skies and settling gently on the earth.

Near Moldy Warp's house stood the magical Christmas tree, as it did every year, with flickering candles, brightly coloured feathers and shells, and icicles and hailstones shining among its branches.

All the creatures of the fields and woods gathered round, admiring the tree, and greeting their friends and neighbours. Rat and his wife and child were among the last to arrive. Once they had stood on the edge of the crowd, not sure if they were welcome. But this Christmas was different. Rat was no longer known for his thieving, but for his skill as a carver and for his health-giving spring water. Above all, he had saved

Grey Rabbit's house from the weasels, and that was
more than enough to make him respected.

> "Holly red and mistletoe white,
> Peace on earth and mercy bright,
> A truce by the tree of candle light,
> Holly red and mistletoe white,"

sang the little company, and Rat felt as if his heart
would burst with happiness.

Little Grey Rabbit's Day Off

Hare was sitting in a comfortable chair by the fire. He felt warm and cosy, and nodded his head as Grey Rabbit talked to him in her quiet voice. Squirrel had just finished brushing her bushy tail with a teazle and was standing by the window watching the wind blow away the last scraps of morning mist.

Little Grey Rabbit began to wash up the breakfast things. She had been the first to get up that morning while the others lay fast asleep in their beds. She had lit the fire and swept the floor and scrubbed the table and cooked the breakfast.

"Grey Rabbit!" called Hare. "Put some more wood on the fire, do!"

"Yes, hurry up Grey Rabbit," grumbled Squirrel, sitting down. "It's getting quite chilly in here."

Little Grey Rabbit sighed. She started to wipe the soap suds off her paws when Hare shouted, "I say, Grey Rabbit. What are you doing? We haven't got all day, you know!"

A big tear trickled down Grey Rabbit's cheek. How mean and selfish Squirrel and Hare could be. For a moment she felt too sad to say anything. Then she heard Squirrel drum her heels impatiently on the floor and call out, "Really, Grey Rabbit, stop being so lazy!"

Grey Rabbit suddenly wiped away her tear. Holding her head high she walked to the pegs near the front door and took down her blue cloak. Then she went into the pantry and packed some good things to eat into a basket.

"Goodbye, Hare. Goodbye, Squirrel," said she. "I am going to visit some friends who will be kinder to me than you are. I am having a day off."

As she shut the door behind her, Hare and Squirrel looked at each other. "Really!" said Squirrel. But Hare leapt out of his easy chair and raced to the window where he was just in time to see Grey Rabbit disappear among the trees at the edge of the wood.

How pleased little Grey Rabbit's friends were to see her at their front door.

"Come in! Come in, Grey Rabbit," said the father rabbit, puffing his pipe. "Sit down, my dear," said his wife, holding the baby in her arms as she got to her feet. "Belinda! Toby! Jessica! Make room for Grey Rabbit by the fire."

"Robert, get some more logs for the fire," called the father. "And put on the kettle, Arabella."

58

Little Grey Rabbit sat by the fire and smiled and smiled. The rabbit children crowded round her, and begged to see what she had in her basket. They gave little cries of joy when she took out the raspberry tartlets, the big slab of home-made toffee and the plum cake with the sugary crust.

Soon, they were drinking steaming cups of tea and eating the delicious food. The baby sat on Grey Rabbit's lap and played with her blue apron. The rabbit children ran about fetching more cups and plates and clearing away the dirty crockery. Then there were games; blind man's buff, and turn the trencher and hunt the thimble.

Grey Rabbit felt like a queen, sitting at the centre of so much fun and happiness and bustle. She wished that the day would go on for ever.

At last she got up to say goodbye. "Oh stay, Grey Rabbit," the children cried. "You can sleep in my bed," said Belinda. "I will get you a fresh brown egg for breakfast," said Robert. The baby just smiled and wriggled his toes.

"No, my dears, I must go home," said Grey Rabbit. "Hare and Squirrel need me to look after them." She looked at the bright little faces around her and sighed. "It *has* been a lovely day," said she. Then she walked rather sadly down the path from the rabbits' cottage, turning to wave to them all before she set off for home.

It was now a sunny spring afternoon, with the new leaves fresh and green on the trees and bushes. Bright flowers peeped from the hedgerows, and the birds sang their merry songs.

Grey Rabbit decided she would walk home through the village to look in at the shop windows. It was a long walk, and soon a chilly wind began to blow. Grey Rabbit paused and put on the bright red shawl that she carried in her bag. She suddenly felt rather daring, as if she was having an adventure. "After all, I am having a day off," she said to herself.

Outside Mrs Bunting's shop, Grey Rabbit met Mrs Webster and Mrs Hedgehog. They were both dressed

in their smartest clothes, and clutched baskets and parcels.

"Why, Grey Rabbit," said Mrs Webster, "fancy seeing you window shopping. Do you like my new hat?" She turned round for Little Grey Rabbit to admire the hat with its crimson ribbons.

"How are Hare and Squirrel?" asked Mrs Hedgehog. She peered at Grey Rabbit and smiled. "I've got a present for my Fuzzypeg in this parcel," she went on. "It's a pair of warm slippers for when he sits by the fire and does his homework of an evening. My husband always says a scollard can't work with cold feet. Are you buying presents for Hare and Squirrel for when they sit by the fire, Grey Rabbit?"

Little Grey Rabbit hung her head. "No," said she in a small, sad voice.

"Well, we'd best be getting on," said Mrs Webster. "Water-rat will be waiting for his supper. I've bought him a nice piece of fish. What are you cooking for supper, Grey Rabbit?"

Little Grey Rabbit hung her head even lower. "I don't know," said she in an even smaller, sadder voice.

As she walked down the path that led to her little house on the edge of the wood, Grey Rabbit felt sure that her two friends would still be cross with her.

Suddenly the door of the house flew open. Hare stood there, his arms open wide. "Grey Rabbit! Dear

Grey Rabbit," called Hare. "Welcome home."

"Yes. Welcome home, dear Grey Rabbit," squeaked
Squirrel. "Where have you been?" The three animals
stood on the doorstep, looking at the wide world
outside, glad to be together again.

What a sight greeted Grey Rabbit when she went
into the kitchen. There was a pile of newly-cut logs by
the blazing fire. The floor had been swept and the
windows sparkled from polishing. The table was laid
for supper, with a pat of yellow butter, a jar of straw-
berry jam and some freshly baked scones. A wonderful
smell of cooking came from the oven.

Grey Rabbit stood smiling at her friends. Hare
helped her take off her red shawl, and Squirrel gave her
a big bunch of cowslips that she had picked in the
fields.

"Forgive us, Grey Rabbit," said Hare. "We have
been selfish for far too long."

"We are sorry, Grey Rabbit," added Squirrel. "From now onwards I shall cook and clean and go shopping, and you can sit all day by the fire."

"And I shall chop the sticks, and wash up the dishes, and . . . and never again stay in bed all morning!" cried Hare, dancing round the room and waving his arms.

Little Grey Rabbit laughed. "I don't want you to do all the work," she said. "I like cooking tasty meals for us, and I enjoy keeping the house neat and tidy.

"But I would like you to help me more, and to think that I might get tired sometimes."

"Yes, of course, Grey Rabbit," they said, nodding their heads. "We agree. You are quite right."

"And," continued Little Grey Rabbit, "I should sometimes like a day off, to visit my friends, or just to walk through the meadows and sniff the fresh flowers and see new things."

"Take a holiday, dear Grey Rabbit," cried Squirrel. "Travel the world like the Wandering Hedgehog," suggested Hare.

"No," replied Little Grey Rabbit, "I don't want that."

She looked round the room. Outside it was getting dark, and she could hear the rooks cawing as they flew back to their nests. Inside was a cheery fire, bright lamps and her two best friends. She felt very happy. It *was* good to be home.

Moldy Warp
Digs for Treasure

Late one night Moldy Warp sat up in bed looking
at a map. It was an ancient piece of parchment,
showing hills and dales and streams and woods. Here
and there words had been written in black ink, but the
map was so old and creased that it was difficult to make
them out.

Moldy Warp turned the map this way and that as the
light from his bedside candle flickered, sending the
shadows dancing across the room.

He had found the map folded up in a small, battered
box that he had dug out from under the roots of the old
hawthorn tree that stood in the middle of Hearthstone
Pasture. He loved delving in the pasture, and admiring
the dark rocks that pushed their solid backs through the
smooth grass. It was a place of mystery, where Mole
had once found a crock of gold by tunnelling deep
beneath its surface into the winding corridors known
only to Brock the Badger. Sometimes an old raven
perched on the rocks and told Moldy Warp of battles
long ago and how the first men and women, clad in the
skins of wild animals, had once made their homes there.

Mole shivered with pleasure and fear at the memory,
and bent his head to the map once more.

"Here's a name I know," said he. "Hearthstone
. . . something." He screwed up his short-sighted eyes.

"Heath," he muttered, "Hearthstone Heath. But there's no such place nowadays. Yet here's the stream, running in the same loop, and the old Roman road, straight as an arrow."

He lifted the map even closer to his eyes. "Yes, it's the same place, but shown as it was hundreds of years ago. Bless me! What's this?"

He sat up even straighter and reached over for his candle. He brought the little yellow flame within a few inches of the map.

"It says 'Here lies treasure', and then there's a cross – next to the biggest rock in Hearthstone Pasture, if I'm not mistaken."

Mole chuckled to himself. "Treasure!" he whispered. "Buried treasure. Gold coins, maybe. Or jewels – rubies and emeralds. I'll go and dig it up tomorrow!"

He blew out his candle and replaced it on his bedside table. Then, clutching the map to his chest, he sank back upon his pillow and went to sleep, smiling contentedly.

Moldy Warp was up at dawn, having spent the night dreaming of mountains of gold and rivers of precious stones. He cooked his mushroom breakfast, but was too excited to sprinkle it with pepper and salt. Then he looked out his work gear, polishing his spade until it shone like silver. Before he went outside he brushed his hair and put on a clean shirt. He gazed at his reflection

in the little bronze mirror and nodded in approval.
"Very smart," said he. "You can't go digging for
buried treasure looking like a tramp. It isn't right."

He locked all of his back doors, hung up his bunch of
green sycamore keys, and emerged, blinking, into the
daylight.

As he began walking over the fields, with his spade
and his bag on his back and the map tucked inside his
waistcoat, Mole thought about the task ahead.

"It'll be buried deep, I'll be bound," he said to
himself. "I'd best get some help."

He cut himself a walking stick from the hedgerow
and made his way towards his sister's house in a nearby
meadow.

His sister came out of her front door when she heard Mole's gruff voice shouting a greeting.

"Why, what brings you here so early, Moldy Warp?" she asked.

"I need a bit of help," replied Mole, gratefully sitting down upon the stool his sister brought him. "I've a mind to dig up some treasure buried deep down in Hearthstone Pasture. I thought your two sons might give me a hand."

His sister shook her head. "They're with their father," she said. "A good distance from here, learning how to mine far underground."

As Moldy Warp got up to leave he caught sight of Hare careering across the meadow, leaping hither and thither.

"Hallo, Hare!" he shouted, making his way towards him.

Hare lolloped up, panting a little.

"Hallo Mole, old chap!" he cried. "Where are you going, looking so spick-and-span?"

"Treasure hunting," replied Moldy Warp, calmly.

Hare stopped dead in his tracks. "Treasure hunting!" he exclaimed. "Oh! Can I go with you, dear Moldy? I love treasure hunting. Last Christmas I found two penny pieces in the plum pudding. Do you know who my famous ancestor was?"

"Columbus Hare," replied Mole, patiently.

"No, not really," said Hare. "Try again."

"The Hare who raced the tortoise in Aesop's Fables?" ventured Mole.

"Perhaps! Perhaps!" said Hare, nodding slowly. "But, really," here he looked round to see if anyone was listening, "it was Blackbeard Hare, the famous pirate!"

"Never heard of him," muttered Mole.

"Never heard of him!" cried Hare. "He robbed the treasure ships in the Spanish Main."

"Never heard of it," commented Mole. "There's no treasure ships where I'm going. It'll be hard work, and plenty of it. Do you mind getting your paws dirty, Hare?"

Hare looked doubtfully at his paws. "Plenty of hard work," he murmured.

He stooped to pick up a dandelion clock. "Goodness me! Is that the time?" he asked. "I'm late again. I'll come treasure hunting another day, Moldy."

"Just as you please, Hare," said Mole, plodding sturdily along.

As he raced off Hare shouted over his shoulder, "I know who'll help you even better than me. Brock the Badger! I'll run ahead and ask him, it'll save your short legs!"

"No, it won't," grumbled Mole, trudging on.

A little later Moldy Warp drew near to the door of Badger's summer residence. Brock was digging potatoes from out of his front garden. Mole was

71

surprised to see that a mother badger sat on the bench outside, holding her baby, while three youngsters played nearby.

Badger came towards him, wiping his paws on his trousers.

"My cousin has come to stay," he explained shyly, shaking Mole by the paw. "I've never been so busy in my life. Those young badgers are into everything, and bright as buttons. Now, what can I do for you, my friend?"

"Oh, nothing," said Mole. "Just passing by."

He smiled at the young badgers and their mother.

"Have you seen Hare lately, Brock?" he asked casually.

Badger shook his head. "Not a whisker," he answered.

Mole felt relieved. "Well, I'd best be going," he announced.

"Going?" cried Brock, putting his great paw on Mole's shoulder. "Whatever for? We have had no visitors since my cousin arrived. You must stay for supper and taste my new potatoes."

"Well," began Mole, but the small badgers crowded round him begging him to stay.

So Moldy Warp did no digging for treasure that day.

The next morning he set off early again, determined to do the work on his own.

But by now the news of the treasure hunt had spread.

Hare had forgotten to tell Badger, but had told every-
body else he had met. Most of those had then told their
friends, and all of them had told their families as soon
as they could.

So when Mole approached the site of the treasure
there was already a fair-sized crowd gathered round
the large black rock.

There were several small rabbits, twitching their
noses as they sniffed the ground, almost as if they hoped
to catch the scent of the treasure. There was a company
of field mice who were passing the time until Mole's
arrival by washing their paws and whiskers in the early
morning dew. Milkman Hedgehog was just arriving
with his yoke across his shoulders and two pails of fresh
milk swinging from it. A couple of bumble-bees buzzed
overhead, and a red admiral butterfly was already
sunning itself upon the smooth surface of the rock.

"Oh dear," sighed Moldy Warp as the little company raised a cheer at his approach. "I didn't want a
crowd like this. I wish I was back in my quiet, dark
home."

He put his bag upon the ground and looked carefully
at the map once more. Then he began to sharpen his
spade. Even as he got ready to dig for the treasure,
Squirrel bounded up, her ribbons flying behind her,
and at the edge of Hearthstone Pasture the fox lurked
behind a clump of trees.

Mole spat on his paws and took up his spade. "The

sooner I dig, the sooner I'll be underground and away from these noisy folk," he thought as the blade cut through the grass.

Soon, a great mound of earth had been thrown up against the black rock. Only by peering into the hole was it possible to see the top of Moldy Warp's head.

Suddenly Mole gave a shout as his spade hit the side of a wooden chest. He tossed a piece of soft, decayed wood out onto the grass.

Hare, who had at last joined the crowd of onlookers, swooped to pick it up.

"It's rotten wood!" he declared, nodding wisely.

"Don't be so foolish, Hare!" snapped Squirrel. "Of course the wood is rotten after all those years underground." She snatched the fragment from him and sniffed it, wrinkling up her nose at the musty, damp smell.

Mole popped his head out of the hole. "I've found it," he said shyly, beaming with pleasure.

"What? Show us! What is it?" cried the creatures, crowding around.

One by one Moldy Warp laid the treasure out before them. There were daggers, dulled with the years but with jewels shining through the soil that clung to their hafts. There were great broad swords with rubies on their handles, and a strange crescent-shaped blade with words of some foreign tongue inscribed upon it. Finally Mole put down two ancient pistols, with curved butts and fine silver barrels.

The crowd of onlookers fell silent.

Milkman Hedgehog bent down to pick up a jewelled dagger. He touched its point gingerly. "It's sharp," he protested. "Sharper than my prickles. I wouldn't like my little Fuzzypeg to play with this." He put it back on the heap of weapons.

"Men use sharp knives to skin animals with," said a rabbit, solemnly. At this, the youngest rabbit began to cry.

Hare snatched up a pistol and waved it about. "Bang! Bang! You're dead," he cried. Squirrel covered her face with her hands, many of the animals shrank back in fear, and the fox, still watching from behind his clump of trees, decided it was time to go home.

Little Grey Rabbit suddenly stepped out from among the crowd of animals. "Dear Moldy Warp," she said timidly. "You have found a very dangerous sort of treasure. We don't need these guns and sharp blades.

They won't make us happier. Let us bury them again, dear Moldy."

"Yes! Put them back in the earth. Bury them again!" chorused the others.

Moldy Warp sighed. "I expect you're right," said he.

So the pistols and swords and daggers were tossed to the bottom of the hole, and Mole shovelled the loose earth over them.

A few weeks later Moldy Warp was sitting outside one of his back doors reading an old newspaper when Grey Rabbit approached. She called out:

"Cuckoo. Cherry-tree.
Moldy Warp, you can't see me."

Mole got up to greet his visitor.

"I've brought you a present, Moldy Warp," said Grey Rabbit. She shyly held out a book. One of its corners was bent, and the gold letters on its spine had almost faded away.

Mole peered at the book. "It's called *Britain's Buried Treasure*," he announced. He turned the pages and saw maps, and pictures of rare and precious things.

"Wise Owl sent it," said Grey Rabbit. "He was sorry to learn that you had to put back the treasure you found."

But Moldy Warp didn't hear her. He was too busy turning the pages of his book, and his eyes were gleaming with pleasure as he made plans for his next search for buried treasure.

The North Wind Doth Blow

The wind was already blowing hard as Milkman Hedgehog made his way home. The trees bent and sighed, and the last autumn leaves flapped and fluttered as the wind snatched at them with its cold fingers.

Hedgehog was glad to see his little round cottage, with its snug thatched roof and the welcoming lamp light at the windows.

Little Fuzzypeg ran to open the door for his father, but the wind rushed in first, whisking round the kitchen and sending some pieces of paper flying from the table.

"Oh, Father!" cried Fuzzypeg. "My homework! I'll never learn all my lessons if the wind takes my sums and poems and tales."

As he bent to pick up the sheets of paper, his father put his back to the door and pushed it shut.

"That'll keep out the wind," said Old Hedgehog. "We can't have it stopping you from larning Wisdom. You'll never be like Wise Owl at this rate, Fuzzypeg."

As they ate their supper the wind continued to howl round the house, rattling the windows and trying to get under the door.

"Are we safe, Husband?" asked Mrs Hedgehog, anxiously. "This morning Postman Robin was telling me he could feel a strange breeze rippling his feathers. 'It'll blow up a treat tonight, Missus,' sez he."

Hedgehog lifted his head from his bowl of milk pudding.

"It's the North Wind, Wife," he replied. "It comes down from the North Pole where it's all snowy and fruzz."

"And where there's polar bears, and Eskimos in igloos, and . . . and reindeer," squeaked Fuzzypeg excitedly.

"What it is to be a scollard!" said Old Hedgehog proudly, stroking his son's spiky head.

That night Mrs Hedgehog insisted that she should have a light in the bedroom. "For comfort, like," said she.

So a candle holder was set on a chair by her bedside, and the little yellow flame flickered, throwing dark shadows here and there onto the white-washed walls.

Old Hedgehog was soon asleep, snoring softly. But Mrs Hedgehog lay awake listening to the wind and worrying.

The North Wind could not sleep either. It grew

wilder and wilder, snapping the dead twigs from the trees and picking up the piles of dried leaves and casting them high into the air. On the bare branches the birds huddled together for warmth and safety, and even the squirrels were shaken out of their winter sleep.

As the wind shrieked round the hedgehogs' cottage, there was suddenly a great crash. Mrs Hedgehog sat up in alarm. "Wake up, Hedgehog!" she cried. "The chimbley's come off. Get up and see what's happened."

Grumbling, Old Hedgehog got out of bed and sleepily made his way towards the window. He rubbed at the glass and peered out.

The trees were swaying violently to and fro as the wind tore at them. Small branches whirled through the air, and it was difficult to see far.

"It's blowing a real old gale out there, Wife," said he. "But our chimbley's safe and sound. Leastways I can't see it a-lying on the ground." He turned to come back to bed.

"But what was that terrible crash?" asked Mrs Hedgehog nervously. "Perhaps our little Fuzzypeg has been blowed out of the window! Oh dear! Oh dear!" She began to cry.

"Don't get all fussed and moithered, my dear," said her husband kindly. "Fuzzypeg's sound asleep, I shouldn't wonder."

Just then, there was another crash from outside. A great shuddering crash that shook the hedgehogs' cottage to its rafters.

Mrs Hedgehog sobbed with fear. "Our house will be blowed away," she said through her tears.

"That was a tree falling," said Old Hedgehog grimly. "Maybe it's Wise Owl's tree, like in the last great storm. I'd best go and see. You'll be safe enough here with Fuzzypeg. Keep warm and cosy."

"Now don't you go by yourself, Husband," wailed Mrs Hedgehog. "You'll be squashed flat by a tree. Your prickles will get bent in the wind."

"Don't fret, my dear," replied Hedgehog. "I know who'll come with me. A wise creature, whose

ancestors have lived hereabouts for a thousand year or more.''

After struggling through the wild night, Old Hedgehog came at last to Badger's house.

He hammered on the thick planks of the front door. But nobody came to answer. He cupped his paws and bellowed and hallooed, but the wind carried the sounds off high into the stormy sky.

Badger was fast asleep, a lantern burning by the side of his bed.

At last, Old Hedgehog opened the door himself and went down the long, twisting corridor to Badger's bedroom.

Badger shook himself awake as Hedgehog knocked on his bedroom door. "Enter!" he called out in a muffled voice.

Soon, he was sitting on the edge of the bed while Old Hedgehog told his tale. When he had heard enough he nodded his great hoary head.

"You were right to come," said he gravely. "I hardly ever have visitors, except sometimes Moldy Warp. We badgers are a race apart. We have lived through many troubles over the centuries. We remember storms and tempests from the time before the Romans came."

Hedgehog looked around him at the treasures of Badger's house. There were shelves full of tiny statues of birds and animals, carved out of coloured stones. There were golden necklaces and bronze brooches, and pots piled high with precious coins and sparkling jewels.

He started as Badger laid his heavy paw on his shoulder.

"Of course we will go and rescue Wise Owl," said Badger. "But first, a little supper. You have woken me from a deep sleep and I am famished. Come."

The two animals ate quickly. Old Hedgehog thought he had never tasted sweeter bread, or drunk such fragrant ale.

A few minutes later Badger was standing outside his front door lifting his lantern high and sniffing the air.

The storm had lessened, though the wind was still blowing hard.

It was not easy for the two animals to make their way through the wood. They had to scramble over fallen

branches, and skirt the trunks of toppled trees, the soil still clinging to their roots. Old Hedgehog was glad he had the Badger's lantern to show him the way, even though the wind several times blew it out.

After a while, they pushed their way through some bushes and there before them was Wise Owl's tree.

"It's still standing!" cried Hedgehog joyfully, and he ran to stand at the base of the beautiful beech.

The tree was swaying in the wind, causing the silver bell by the front door to tinkle. Hedgehog pulled on the long cord and the bell rang loudly.

Wise Owl put his head out of his door. His feathers seemed a little ruffled.

"Too-whit, too-whoo! What's the matter with you?" he hooted.

"We thought your tree might be blown down!" shouted Hedgehog.

Owl blinked at him crossly. "My tree is perfectly safe," said he. "It's been a trifle windy in the night, but it's blown the cobwebs out of the corners and aired my goose-feather bed. Go away!"

The Badger stepped forward and held up his lantern. "Now don't be hasty, my dear fellow," he called. "We've just come to make sure you're safe and sound. We can't afford to lose a wise creature like you."

"Humph!" said Owl. "Very grateful, I'm sure." And he turned and went inside his house.

Hedgehog gazed up, open-mouthed. In a few

moments Owl reappeared and tossed something down.

The gale had almost died away by now, but the little book fluttered and spun this way and that before it landed on the ground.

Old Hedgehog picked it up and turned it over. He could not make head nor tail of the words upon its cover.

"It's a useful book," hooted Owl, scornfully. "*The History of Storm and Tempest through the Ages.* Take it home and give it to Fuzzypeg. Now, goodbye!"

With that, he slammed shut his little green door and went back to bed.

"Well, I'm blessed," said Old Hedgehog, turning to Badger.

But Badger had vanished.

Hedgehog scratched his head. "Gone back for his winter sleep I expect," said he to himself.

The wind had almost ceased, and the first light of day was seeping through the battered wood.

"The calm *after* the storm," muttered Hedgehog contentedly. He put the little book into the pocket of his smock, and returned to his cottage to get ready for milking.

Fuzzypeg exclaimed with delight as he sat on his father's knee and turned the pages of the book. "And the chimbley stayed on, Husband!" called Mrs Hedgehog happily as she poured out the tea. But Old Hedgehog had fallen asleep by the fire.

The Fox
Goes Hunting

The Fox lay dozing in bed late one morning. In fact, it was past midday before he finally woke up.

For a while he lay under the blankets trying to remember his dreams. They had been wonderful dreams, full of fat hens on their nests and tender young rabbits romping in the meadows.

Lazily, the fox licked his lips with his long red tongue. "Is rabbit best roasted or stewed?" he thought. "Then there's jugged hare. That's delicious with redcurrant jelly. But, there again, nothing can beat a plump roasted chicken with stuffing and bread sauce."

He suddenly felt very hungry. He got out of bed and put on his coat that he had carelessly flung onto a stool the night before.

Although the Fox looked smart when he went out of doors, wearing his coat and scarf, quite a gentleman really, his house was very untidy. It was a ruined mill house beside a stream and the Fox did not take good care of it. The pictures hung crookedly on the walls, there were piles of feathers in the corners and half-eaten bones under the bed. Thick dust lay everywhere, and the spiders had spun their cobwebs over some of the windows.

The Fox went into the kitchen and opened the pantry door. There was nothing to eat there except a half-empty jar of redcurrant jelly and two uncooked potatoes.

He turned aside angrily and went outside, slamming the front door hard behind him.

As he walked silently through the Bilberry Wood, stepping carefully to avoid breaking the dry sticks underfoot, his nose quivered as he sniffed for the scent of some animal he might catch.

A few mice scuttled away amid the dead leaves and a young hedgehog disappeared among the bracken, but these were not what the Fox was seeking.

He stepped out of the shade of the wood and straightened his red jacket.

Crossing the field at the edge of the wood was a familiar figure wearing a blue coat, twisting this way and that to talk to the birds or to pick a wild flower.

"Halloo!" called the Fox, putting his paws on either side of his mouth to make his voice carry.

Hare stopped dead in his tracks, and the Fox loped easily towards him.

"Hare! My dear chap!" exclaimed the Fox as he approached. "Fancy seeing you. What a piece of luck!"

Hare sniffed the strange odour that came from the Fox, a smell that awoke uncomfortable memories of other meetings with the red-coated gentleman, and he began to tremble.

"You see, Hare," said the Fox, placing a paw on the quaking animal's shoulder, "I need some advice."

"Advice, Mr Fox?" quavered Hare. "Oh, I'm no good at giving advice. Go and ask Wise Owl. He's always got plenty of advice."

"No," said the Fox, gazing intently at Hare. "It's you I wanted."

Hare nodded dumbly.

"What I want . . . to ask you," continued the Fox, "is whether stewed rabbit is tastier than roast rabbit? Or perhaps you prefer jugging to either?"

Desperately Hare put his paw into his pocket to find his watch.

"Tick Tack, Tick Tack" went the watch as he began to pull it out.

The Fox jumped back. "What's that? A bomb?" he exclaimed. "I don't like ticking noises."

"Shall I show you, Mr Fox?" asked Hare innocently.

"No, thank you," replied the Fox hastily. "I've just remembered. I've got to pay a visit to a dear friend of mine," and he moved away.

"Roast fox is best!" shouted Hare boldly as the Fox disappeared into the Bilberry Wood.

"The Fox is out hunting," he thought as he lolloped

away. "I'd best warn the creatures hereabouts."

A few minutes later, Hare knocked loudly on the door of a nearby cottage where a family of rabbits lived. The mother was stirring some soup, ready to feed her husband and three children, when Hare burst in.

"The Fox! Stewed rabbit! Roast jugs!" he gasped, flopping down in a chair. He sniffed the cooking and sat up again. "Oh, is that vegetable soup?" he asked. "Delicious! Thank you. I don't mind if I do."

The father rabbit stood up. "What's all this, Hare?" he asked sternly. "Is the Fox out hunting?"

"He's coming," replied Hare, waving his paw towards the door. "Soon. He's famished. He wants stews and roast jugs."

"What's roast jugs?" asked the smallest rabbit looking up from her doll's cradle, but before anyone could reply her mother snatched her up and held her close.

"Shut the windows! Lock the door!" cried the father rabbit, bundling Hare outside. "That'll keep the Fox out. Thank you, Hare, and good luck!"

"A pity about that delicious vegetable soup," murmured Hare as he galloped off.

Within the next hour, Hare managed to warn many animals and birds that the Fox was out hunting. Doors were bolted, windows locked, and youngsters called in from play.

When the Fox came prowling up to the cottages and houses where he hoped to find his food he discovered that he could not get in. Although he hammered on a few doors, and tried to prise some windows open, he had no luck. So he became more and more hungry, and more and more cross.

Hare arrived home out of breath, but full of himself.

"Grey Rabbit! Squirrel!" he shouted as he shut the door behind him. "I'm a hero. I've warned our neighbours that the Fox is looking for his dinner. Do you think I'll get a medal?"

But Grey Rabbit went quickly round the house shutting the windows, and Squirrel looked out two of her sharpest knitting needles and clutched them tight.

Unfortunately, there was one place that Hare did not

visit, and that was the farmyard. Perhaps he knew that the cart-horse, the cows and the pigs had nothing to fear from the Fox. Perhaps he thought that the farm dog would chase his old enemy away if he came near. Probably, though, Hare clean forgot, so anxious was he to race home and tell Grey Rabbit and Squirrel the news.

The Speckledy Hen was standing at the top of the little ladder that led to her house when the Fox drew near the farmyard. Below her was her friend the Black Hen who had come to show off her brood of yellow chicks.

"What lovely chicks, to be sure," said the Speckledy Hen. "And so alike. I can't tell whether they take more after you or their father."

"Well, they're not like either of us yet," replied the Black Hen, looking fondly at her brood as they scurried round her. "But when their feathers start growing I expect they'll be black."

"Black feathers are beautiful," observed the Speckledy Hen. "But, then, so are brown, or white."

"I always say," replied her friend, "that it doesn't matter what colour their feathers are, as long as they're healthy."

"And happy," said the Speckledy Hen, putting her head on one side.

"And helpful," remarked the Black Hen scratching in the dust.

The two hens might have stayed there gossiping for hours but for the sudden appearance of the Fox.

The farm dog was out in the fields rounding up some sheep, and none of the farm workers was nearby, so the Fox had been able to sidle up to the hen-house unobserved.

The Speckledy Hen saw him plain enough though.

"Help! The Fox!" she squawked. "Murder! Help!"

The Black Hen gathered up her brood and squeezed through the small, low door that led into the hen-house at ground level.

The Speckledy Hen tried to pull up the ladder upon which she had been standing, but it was too heavy, and she gave up, gasping for breath.

The Fox ran to the ladder and gazed up at her with a leer.

"Good afternoon, Missus," said he. "Your eyes are as bright as ever, I see."

"Shoo! Be off with you, you bad creature!" shrieked the Hen.

"Won't you invite me inside, Missus?" asked the Fox politely. "Then I could admire your soft, silky feathers."

"Shoo! Off with you," cried the Hen.

"Now, don't be so unkind," replied the Fox, and he began to climb up the ladder.

The Speckledy Hen shrieked and cried out. She took off her green bonnet and threw it in the Fox's face.

She cackled and called. In fact, she made such a hullaballoo that the Cock heard and came flying over to see what was wrong.

He swooped at the Fox, pecking at his head, and trying to scratch him with his sharp claws.

The Fox snapped hither and thither with his strong teeth, but he could not catch the Cock.

At last he gave up, and slunk out of the farmyard as quietly and quickly as he could.

"Well done, my brave Speckledy!" cried the Cock, looking up at where the little hen stood, her feathers raised and her eyes gleaming.

Soon the chicks and the Black Hen came out from their hiding place and peace returned to the farmyard.

The Fox slowly made his way back to the Bilberry Wood.

"A hen with a temper like that," he said to himself, "would have been very tough to eat. I'm glad I couldn't catch her."

But the thought of eating anything at all reminded him how hungry he was, and he turned aside and made for his sister's house under the roots of an old oak tree.

His sister came out to greet him, wearing her apron.

"What's for supper?" asked the Fox eagerly.

"There's a good, rich stew," answered his sister.

"With plenty of bones in it."

"No jugged hare?" inquired the Fox.

"There was a few days ago," replied his sister briskly. "But the little'uns have eaten it all up."

The Fox sighed. Then his keen nose caught the scent of the stew bubbling away over the fire. He brightened up.

"I needn't have spent all that time hunting, after all," said he, as he followed his sister into the kitchen.

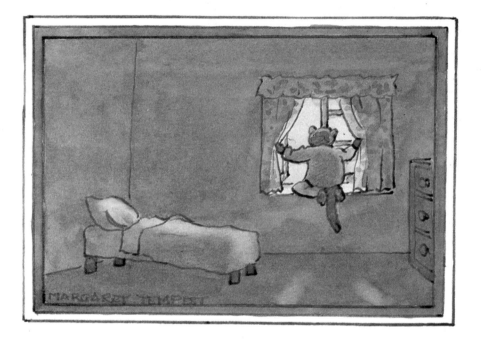

A Midsummer Night's Party

It was the morning of Midsummer's Day. The sun had risen very early and was gently warming the earth beneath it. Everywhere the creatures of the wildwood, the meadows and the riverbank were stirring. Butterflies were already fluttering among the flowers, the birds were calling out as they searched for food, and only the animals that hunted at night were still asleep.

So beautiful was the morning, and so soft were the colours of the countryside, that few could think ill of their neighbours or nurse old hatreds.

Even the young weasel who was a nephew of bad William, Winkie and Winnie Weasel felt kindly as he knelt on his window sill and opened the curtains. "What a lovely morning," said he to himself, and he bared his sharp teeth, not in a snarl, but in a smile.

On the other side of the valley, Postman Robin knocked on the door of little Grey Rabbit's house. "Good morning, mam," he said when Grey Rabbit opened the door. "It's a rare Midsummer's morning. Do you have any messages to be delivered? Milkman Hedgehog told me you might have some."

Hare came to the door, still in his dressing-gown. "Aren't there any letters for me, Postman?" he asked, yawning. "No presents from my admirers?"

"It's not your turn for presents, Hare," called

Squirrel from inside the kitchen. "Today is Grey Rabbit's birthday."

"Yes," said little Grey Rabbit. "But it's also Midsummer's Day. A special day, when all creatures should help each other and draw close together."

"Is that why you've written out all those invitations?" asked Hare turning and running into the kitchen. He returned in a moment carrying a bundle of shiny, dark green holly leaves in his paws.

"Ouch!" he cried, dropping several on the floor. "They're too prickly."

Grey Rabbit took them from him, and calmly handed them to the Robin.

The postman cocked his head to one side and read what the invitations said.

> "Come to a Midsummer's Night Party,
> By the Great Rock in Hearthstone Pasture.
> Dancing by the light of the full moon.
> Wear masks or Fancy Dress."

"No RSVP, mam?" asked the Robin.

"What's RSVP? I've forgotten," muttered Hare, looking puzzled.

" 'Reply Soon Very Politely', of course, Hare!" snapped Squirrel.

"Oh, I thought it meant 'Rat Shan't Visit Party'," said Hare meekly.

"But there's no time for RSVPs today," said Grey
Rabbit quickly. "And Rat shall certainly come. No
creature shall be banned from our Midsummer's Night
Party."

"Not even the Fox?" asked Hare nervously.

"Not even the Fox," replied little Grey Rabbit
firmly. "Perhaps he'll bring some of his games, like
Noughts and Crosses."

"Or Forfeits," suggested Squirrel.

Hare was about to protest, when Grey Rabbit said,
"Thank you very much, Postman. Deliver those
invitations as quickly as you can."

The Robin flew off, fastening the buckle of his bag.
He darted hither and thither, popping the invitations
through letter boxes in doors, into holes in the ground,
or into crannies in trees.

He was tired when at last he returned to his nest. "It's

lucky we robins are quick on the wing," said he to his wife as he hung up his empty postbag.

The invitations to a Midsummer's Night Party caused a great stir.

When Moldy Warp visited his sister for tea there was talk of little else.

The young moles could barely eat their bread and jam for the excitement. "What will you wear, Uncle?" they asked.

Moldy Warp thought for a little. "I always turn out spick and span for these occasions," he replied slowly. "A guest owes that to his hostess, especially when it's her birthday, too. Wait and see."

Wise Owl could not think of what fancy dress to wear. He turned out his cupboards, and moved his piles

of books, but he was unable to find the answer.

At last he flew off to ask his mother's advice.

Old Mrs Owl clutched her shawl about her, and blinked rather crossly at him as he alighted on the branch next to her blue front door.

"What's all this about parties?" she asked, irritably. "Is it a Drinks Party? I hope it's not one of those All-night Parties. You might meet some young lady owl there and fall in love. That would never do, not at your time of life."

"It's a Fancy Dress Midsummer's Night Party," replied Wise Owl humbly. "I'm sure you've no cause for alarm, Mother. In any case, you're invited too."

"Well, I shan't go!" said his mother. "All those

falderals and flirting. It's not right." All the same, she straightened her shawl and began to preen her feathers.

As the time approached for the party, many families hurried to make their masks or to put on fancy dress.

"What shall I go as, Mother?" asked little Fuzzy-peg, but Mrs Hedgehog couldn't provide an answer.

"Why not go as a scollard?" suggested Old Hedge-hog when he came home. "You could put on a black gown and a mortar board cap and carry a book."

"But where will we get a mortar board cap?" wailed Mrs Hedgehog. So, in the end, Fuzzypeg dressed up as a pin cushion.

In his house on the river bank, Water-rat was trying on various disguises while Mrs Webster fussed around him, picking up the clothes that he carelessly dropped on the floor.

"Do you think I should dress up as a pirate, Mrs Webster, or as an admiral?" asked Water-rat. "Of course, admirals don't wear frilly collars."

"I'm sure I don't know, sir," grumbled Mrs Webster, puffing as she stooped to pick up a three-cornered admiral's hat that had been in Water-rat's family for over a hundred years.

"A pirate, I think," said Water-rat, pausing to glance at his reflection in the weather-glass that hung on the wall. "Then I can wear an eye-patch *and* a frilly collar."

That evening as fathers came home from work, they

were met by excited children bearing news of the party and demanding to know if they could go.

Even Rat, as he trudged home carrying his scythe, was greeted by the squeaks of the young rat in his cradle.

"Well, yes, I suppose we can go," said Rat, doubtfully, as he sat down. "But it's Grey Rabbit's birthday today. I must make her a present."

He pulled a piece of bone out of his coat pocket and began gnawing at it. Tiny white splinters fell on his knees as he worked.

At last he held out his handiwork for his family to admire. It was a delicate carving of Grey Rabbit herself, with her basket on her arm.

"Really, I don't know how you do it, Rat," said

his wife, smiling. "I only hope our little 'un takes after you."

"Oh, it's nothing much," replied Rat, slipping the little carving into his pocket. But all the same, he blushed and wriggled his toes with pleasure.

The sun was still shining warmly on the great black rock in Hearthstone Pasture as the guests began to gather for the party. Among the first to arrive were the Hedgehog family. "I has to get up at daybreak to milk the cows," explained Old Hedgehog from behind his mask. "So we can't stay for all the merry-making. Early to bed, early to rise, is what I always says."

"But couldn't you get up an hour before daybreak so as to have a rest, Father?" squeaked Fuzzypeg from within his pincushion disguise. "Then you wouldn't be tired for the milking."

Hedgehog scratched his head. "Thank'ee, Fuzzypeg," he answered. "They say a little larning is a dangerous thing, but you're too deep for me, my boy." And he bent to offer cups of milk from his pail to a family of field mice.

The old hawthorn tree beside the black rock had been decorated with garlands of flowers threaded on string, with bunches of ribbon-grass and fans of bright birds' feathers that turned in the gentle evening breeze.

As if pulled by some magic spell, little groups of animals and birds gathered round the ancient tree. Water-rat caused some anxiety when he arrived dressed as a pirate, a patch over one eye and a cutlass at his side. So did the Fox when he stepped out swiftly from behind the rock wearing his red hunting-jacket. "It's fancy dress, already," he explained. The Speckledy Hen came, struggling with a large basket containing a birthday cake for Grey Rabbit, and baked from her own eggs. Wise Owl flew down, followed by his mother who tried to pretend that she had no intention of enjoying herself. Even the three wicked weasels turned up, though they spent the first half hour or so squabbling with one another, and eyeing each new arrival hungrily.

Last of all came little Grey Rabbit, Squirrel and Hare, accompanied by Moldy Warp in his dark Sunday suit.

Then there was much talking and joking and merrymaking. Coloured candles were set upon the cake, and many presents, mostly home-made, were given to Grey Rabbit for her birthday.

Games were played, and riddles asked. Fuzzypeg was awarded the prize for the best fancy dress. Squirrel won loud applause for the prettiest mask and Winnie Weasel for the most frightening one – though her brother Winkie whispered loudly that it wasn't a mask at all.

The sun set at last in a rich, red haze. As darkness fell the Fox made his excuses and slipped away into the shadows. "I have to meet a man about a dog," said he. The remaining creatures laughed and sang and danced, celebrating the longest day and the shortest night of the year.

Finally, tired but happy, they trooped home by moonlight. Soon they were tucked up in bed and peacefully asleep.

But even as the last bedside candle was blown out, the sun was once more rising to lighten up the eastern sky.

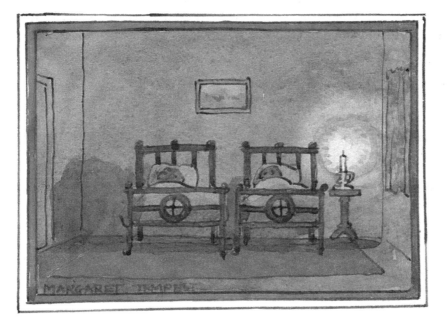

Hare Runs Wild

One day Hare woke up much earlier than usual. It was hardly light yet, and it felt quite cold when he sniffed the air. But although he was often the last to get up for breakfast, today was different.

He leapt out of his bed, making the wooden floorboards creak as he landed on them. He hurriedly put on his clothes and tip-toed out onto the landing.

From Squirrel's bedroom came the sound of snoring. Hare peeped round Grey Rabbit's door and saw a little figure huddled under the bedclothes fast asleep.

Hare slipped down the stairs, grabbed an apple from the bowl on the kitchen table, and went outside wrapping his red and white muffler round his neck.

The wind was blowing hard, whistling through the trees, and shaking the new, bright green leaves on their branches.

Hare began dancing through the fields, skipping and tripping, round and round like a spinning top.

He became so dizzy that he didn't notice Milkman Hedgehog plodding along towards him carrying his milk pails.

Hare whirled round, waving his arms and feeling very wild and excited, when – crash! – he found himself tumbling on the damp grass. Opposite him, Old Hedgehog was sitting on the ground, rubbing his spiky head.

"Mind out, Mr Hare," he grumbled. "Why are you in such a harum-scarum-hurry? You've spilt half of my milk I'm taking to my customers. What'll they have for breakfast now?"

Hare leaped to his feet. "I'm sorry, Hedgehog!" he cried. "But I can't help it. I'm a mad March Hare, you see, and I'm running wild."

Old Hedgehog stared at him. "But it's the end of April, Mr Hare," said he. "It seems to me, you're a bit moithered and muddled."

"Oh, I don't care," replied Hare airily, pulling the hedgehog to his feet and straightening his smock. "I'm having an adventure. I'm running wild."

"Tell Grey Rabbit!" he called over his shoulder as he raced off.

"Running wild," muttered Old Hedgehog to himself, shaking his head. "What's the point of that, I'd like to know?"

Many hours later Hare walked down the path of his Aunt Matilda's house. He felt tired and hungry, and had enough of running wild – for the moment anyway.

His aunt tut-tutted when she heard what he had done.

"Grey Rabbit and Squirrel will miss you," said she. "You should be more thoughtful, Hare."

"I can't help myself," replied Hare. "I'm Columbus Hare, the famous traveller." But secretly, inside, he began to feel ashamed.

His aunt frowned at him as she put the tea upon the

table, and when he had finished his meal Hare decided to go home.

Little Grey Rabbit and Squirrel jumped up when he came into the kitchen. "Oh, Hare!" cried Grey Rabbit. "We have been worried about you, even though Milkman Hedgehog told us that he had seen you." But Squirrel tossed her head, and smoothed her ribbons and said nothing at all.

A few days later Hare did it again. It was Sunday, and before the others were awake he put on his red coat, crept down the stairs, and vanished into the morning mist.

MARGARET TEMPEST

After a while Hare came to the edge of Ash Wood. As he ran under the rustling leaves of its grey trees, he remembered his first great adventure, years ago, when he had called upon old Toad in the bog in the middle of the wood.

Soon Hare saw Toad's small house, perched on an island. Its roof was neatly thatched with rushes, and the bright blue paint of the door and windows was reflected in the still waters of the bog.

As Hare waded through the muddy water with his coat tails turned up, the door of the little house opened.

There stood old Toad, clad in his yellow breeches and green coat. His cheeks were even more wrinkled than Hare remembered them, and his eyes still shone like lamps.

"Who's there?" he boomed. "Why, bless me, if it isn't Hare. What are you doing, so far from Grey Rabbit's house over the valley? Do you want medicines? Or a bottle of my famous Venom for some Dangerous Visitors?"

Hare struggled out of the bog and stood before the wise creature. Water trickled down his legs, and he felt awkward.

"I'm running wild," said he.

There was a silence as the Toad gazed at him intently.

"Come in, Hare, come in," he said at last, throwing open the little blue door.

Stooping, Hare followed him over the cool flagstones of the hall and past the courtyard with its clear, sparkling fountain.

Soon, Hare was sitting at Toad's table, while the housekeeper and two frogs brought them red wine, pies and saffron cake. Toad dipped his piece of cake into the wine to moisten. it. "I have no teeth, Hare," he explained.

It was a delicious meal, and Hare was stretching out his legs and feeling comfortable, when Toad suddenly spoke.

"What's all this nonsense about running wild, Hare?" he asked sternly. "You should know better."

Hare was about to explain that he was really Columbus Hare, when he caught Toad's eye and thought better of it.

"Last time you visited me I gave you presents, Hare," continued Toad. "But this time I will only give you some advice – go home, and don't be a worry to Grey Rabbit any more."

Hare quailed before the wise creature, and soon he made his excuses and scuttled home.

You might think that was the end of Hare's adventures. Hare thought so himself. But about a week later he felt the old urge to run away and dance across the fields and off he went again.

After a delightful day spent whirling and prancing about the countryside, nodding to rabbits and calling to birds, Hare felt tired but happy.

He walked through a spinney of fir trees singing loudly, and stepped into a little clearing.

Straight in front of him was an ugly little house made of dark and dingy pieces of wood. A weasel stood outside pumping water, while his wife sat on the doorstep knitting.

The weasel at once stopped his work and came up to Hare showing his sharp teeth in a crooked smile.

"Well, if it isn't Mr Hare, come a-visiting," he said. "You're just in time for supper."

"Oh, no, don't bother about me," stammered Hare. "I'm late already. I'll be · off, if you don't mind."

"But I *do* mind, Mr Hare," said the weasel with a leer. He pinched Hare's arm and called out to his wife, "Put on the cooking pot, my dear. And sharpen the carving knife."

The terrified Hare pulled his arm free from the weasel's clutches and ran back through the fir trees as fast as the wind.

He didn't stop until he reached the first friendly

house, where Old Jonathan Rabbit, the schoolmaster, lived.

Jonathan sat him down, and made him a cup of herbal tea, and listened to the tale of his narrow escape. But when he eventually suggested that his guest should go home Hare began to shake all over.

"I can't!" he cried. "I daren't! Don't send me out to be eaten by foxes and weasels, Jonathan."

"Why, whatever happened to Columbus Hare the great explorer?" asked Old Jonathan gently. But Hare just groaned and continued to tremble like a leaf.

So Jonathan sent word to Grey Rabbit. Soon she was walking down his path, wearing her red shawl and carrying her basket.

Jonathan greeted her at the door, and Hare rushed out when he saw the homely little figure approaching. "Grey Rabbit! Grey Rabbit!" he called. "Oh, I am so glad to see you. The weasels nearly caught me. I will never run wild again, not even in March. Oh, Grey Rabbit!"

But little Grey Rabbit just hugged him and told him that he was quite safe. Then, having thanked Old Jonathan, she led a sadder and a wiser Hare back to the little house at the edge of the wood.

MARGARET TEMPEST

Squirrel
Makes an Important Choice

One Summer morning Squirrel was sitting at the breakfast table and feeling rather cross. Little Grey Rabbit had already gone out to see if the Speckledy Hen had three fresh brown eggs to spare for their supper. Hare was still in his dressing-gown, and talking rather loudly.

"Did I ever tell you the story of my escape from the weasels, Squirrel?" he asked, waving his knife in the air.

"Yes, you have," replied Squirrel. "Ten times at least."

But Hare carried on as if he had not heard a word. "It was an amazing adventure," said he, spreading some butter on his toast. "Of course, I am a born adventurer and explorer. But now I think I am a born escaper, too."

"And still a born boaster," muttered Squirrel to her teacup.

"You have to be brave to escape from the weasels," continued Hare. "And strong," he added, nodding contentedly.

"And conceited," whispered Squirrel.

"And daring," said Hare, looking dreamily out of the window at the clothes fluttering on the washing line. "In fact," he went on, "I shouldn't be surprised if I'm not the most daring Hare in history." He kept on staring out of the window as if he could see his adventures happening all over again.

"What do you think, Squirrel?" he asked at last, turning towards her and smiling his self-satisfied smile.

But Squirrel's chair was empty.

Hare jumped up, almost knocking over the teapot.

"Squirrel!" he called. "Where are you? I haven't finished telling you about my escape, and how I raced away like the North Wind."

There was no answer.

Hare looked under the table, and behind his rocking chair. He called up the stairs, and peeped through the kitchen window. At last, he shrugged his shoulders, sat down, and buttered another piece of toast.

Meanwhile, Squirrel was far away, making her way towards the great beech tree where her cousin, the Red Squirrel, lived.

"That foolish Hare won't dare to follow me here," said she to herself. "He's frightened of Red Squirrel because he's big and bold and shouts at strangers."

As she neared the beech tree Squirrel paused. A little face was peering at her from a window. It wasn't her cousin. In fact, Squirrel had no idea who it was. Then the window was pulled shut and the face disappeared.

Squirrel straightened her ribbons, smoothed her yellow dress, and knocked on the door.

Nobody came to open it. She knocked again, and

then let herself in.

There, in a corner of the living room sat a young squirrel eating his breakfast.

"Who are you?" asked Squirrel. "And don't you know you should stand up when a lady comes into the room?" She tossed her head, and clicked her tongue disapprovingly.

The young squirrel looked down shyly at the table-cloth. He seemed about to burst into tears.

"And where is my cousin, the Red Squirrel?" demanded Squirrel, appearing not to notice his sadness.

129

"Uncle Red's gone out," said the young squirrel sadly to the table-cloth.

"Oh, indeed," said Squirrel, opening wide her eyes. "And what, pray, are you doing here?"

The young squirrel looked at her for the first time. "I'm an orphan," said he mournfully. "Men with guns shot my mother and my father, but Uncle Red rescued me and said I could come and live with him."

"Oh, indeed," said Squirrel, gasping with surprise. "Well, well!"

She looked around the room. "This will never do," she said. "Bits of food on the floor and cobwebs in the corners. What is your Uncle Red thinking of?"

For the next hour she swept the floors with the besom, dusted the furniture and polished the windows until they sparkled. She made the sad young squirrel sandwiches, and packed him off to make friends with the birds and animals of the wood outside.

Then she put a cloth on the table in the sitting room, and baked a cherry cake and some currant buns.

When at last her cousin, the big Red Squirrel, came back the kettle was boiling and his home shone like a new pin.

"Squirrel! Dear cousin, Squirrel," said he as he sipped his tea. "Not even Grey Rabbit could clean and polish and bake better than you."

Squirrel nibbled on a small slice of cake and looked modestly at her yellow cuffs. "True, very true," she

said in her smallest, softest voice.

"Come and live with me, dear Squirrel," continued her cousin, brushing some crumbs from the lapels of his blue coat. "Be my companion and my housekeeper. Be another mother to my poor, sad nephew."

Squirrel turned her head aside and blushed.

The big Red Squirrel leaned across and put his large paw on top of her dainty one. "Nobody could be kinder or more generous than you," he said.

"True, very true," said Squirrel, still in her smallest, softest voice.

"Think about it, dear cousin," said the Red Squirrel.

All the way home Squirrel could think of nothing else.

When Squirrel told her two friends all about it, Hare danced around the kitchen, spluttering with rage.

"How can you think of such a thing, Squirrel!" he cried. "Who would climb up the trees to bring us walnuts in the autumn? Who would fetch us honey from the wild bees' nests?"

He stamped his foot. "What do you think, Grey Rabbit?" he cried.

Little Grey Rabbit sat in silence for a while. Then she lifted her head and looked at Squirrel.

"We would miss you, dear Squirrel," said she sadly. "But the Red Squirrel does need help, and he is your cousin."

"Thank you, Grey Rabbit," whispered Squirrel.

"Cousin! Fiddlesticks!" shouted Hare. "It's us you should be thinking of!"

"It's you, you mean!" snapped Squirrel.

"Let us all think it over," said Grey Rabbit quietly.

Weeks went by, and still Squirrel couldn't decide what to do. Hare sulked and fussed, but little Grey Rabbit said nothing at all.

The summer faded. The harvest was gathered in, and the leaves began to turn red and golden upon the trees. Squirrel visited her cousin often, but still she couldn't decide what to do.

At last she made up her mind. As she approached the beech tree where the Red Squirrel lived she saw his little nephew climbing through the branches, laughing and chattering with other young squirrels.

Inside the great tree trunk she found her cousin

busy storing away nuts for the winter. The room was neat and tidy, and a pot of soup was bubbling on the stove.

Squirrel took her cousin by the paw and led him out onto the branch by the upper door.

She pointed with her red umbrella to the branches overhead. Shrieks of joy came from the little squirrel as he chased his friends.

"Dear cousin," she said gently, "you don't need me to come and live with you. Your nephew is happy now, and you are looking after him and your home better than I could do.

"The truth is," she continued sadly, "I don't really like too much cooking and sweeping and cleaning. I'd rather put on my best dress and go and admire my reflection in the pond."

The Red Squirrel opened his mouth to say something, but no words came out. In the end he just nodded, and squeezed Squirrel's paw very hard indeed.

So Squirrel didn't leave home after all. She went back to the little house at the edge of the wood and slipped into her chair by the fire as quietly as she could. Hare was swaying back and forth in his rocking chair, his eyes closed, and humming a tune to himself. But little Grey Rabbit, who was sitting at the table darning a sock, caught Squirrel's eye and smiled a deep, secret smile.

Water-Rat
Saves the Day

Water-rat was strolling down his garden path early one morning, whistling a sea shanty and feeling very happy. The sun was shining on his riverside garden, and a gentle breeze was blowing over the flowering rushes and the water-mint.

"What a beautiful day" said Water-rat to himself. "I'll put a picnic into my boat, the 'Saucy Nancy', and invite some of my friends to join me for a day on the river. Perhaps Grey Rabbit will come, and Squirrel. Hare might choose to stay at home, though. The last time we went on a boat he fell into the water and caught a cold."

Water-rat chuckled softly at the memory and walked back to his house for breakfast.

Soon he was sitting at the table with Mrs Webster, his stout housekeeper, spreading some lily-bud jam on his bread.

"We shall want plenty of watercress sandwiches, Mrs Webster," he said, daintily flicking a crumb from his velvet jacket. "And pack in some lobster patties, and some . . ."

But Mrs Webster never heard what else she had to prepare, for Water-rat suddenly stopped speaking and cocked his head to one side.

"Why, what is it, sir?" asked Mrs Webster.

"Shush!" replied Water-rat. "Can't you hear it?"

They both listened in silence.

From far, far away came the sound of dogs barking.

Water-rat leapt to his feet. "That noise," he cried. "It's otter hounds, baying for blood!" He went to the window, and looked out anxiously.

Suddenly a kingfisher landed on the window ledge in a flurry of bright blue feathers. "Look out, Rat," it cried. "I've seen them. Three otter hounds. They've escaped from the pack and are running wild. Dangerous, hungry creatures. Listen!"

Mrs Webster put her paws over her ears, as the baying grew louder. "Escaped hounds," said Water-rat grimly. "I must warn the folk of the river bank that danger is approaching."

"But, sir," protested Mrs Webster, "don't go outside. You might get killed. Oh, sir!"

But Water-rat was racing towards his boat-house, waving farewell to the kingfisher as he ran. In a minute or two he was sitting in the 'Saucy Nancy' and pulling on her slender, scarlet oars.

Mrs Webster rushed out of the front door as he

turned the boat round in midstream.

"Get back in the house!" Water-rat shouted. "Pull the reeds over the door, and hide yourself."

"Good luck, sir!" Mrs Webster called after him tearfully, but Water-rat never heard as he bent to the oars and the 'Saucy Nancy' flew through the water.

Swallows swooped over the boat as it sped upstream. "Lovely day, Ratty," they twittered cheerfully. But Water-rat simply raised his head and shouted, "Danger! Hunting dogs are coming! Tell the birds and animals of the river bank to hide. Quick about it!"

Away flew the swallows, faster than the wind, raising the alarm in their shrill, piping voices.

Soon Water-rat was at Otter's home, tucked under the roots of a great willow tree. Once he had peeped into the house to see how many were in the family, and what kind of furniture they had, and had then fled when the young otter had seen him and cried out.

But now he forgot his fear, leaped out of his boat, and, seeing the door was ajar, pushed it open.

Mrs Otter looked up in alarm from her knitting, and the young otter dropped his wooden bricks in fright. Mr Otter took his pipe out of his mouth and showed his sharp white teeth.

"Hounds!" gasped Water-rat.

Mr Otter stood up. "Where?" he asked sternly.

"Coming," said Water-rat pointing to the doorway. "Up the river. You must hide."

Within a few minutes the Otter family had slipped away from their warm hearth and into a dark, damp tunnel deep under the roots of the willow tree.

Next Water-rat turned aside into the stream leading to the swamp in the middle of Ash Wood. After a while the 'Saucy Nancy' got stuck in the sluggish waters, and

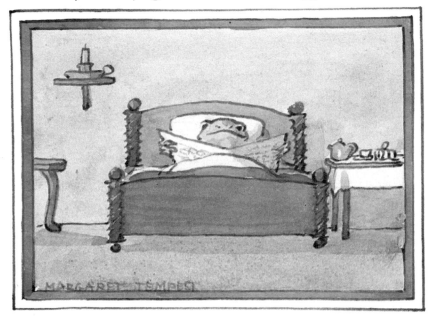

he had to leap out and wade towards Toad's small, neat house.

When finally he reached the front door his fine velvet coat and his frilly white cuffs were spattered with mud, but Water-rat was in too much of a hurry to fuss over that. Old Toad was lying in bed reading his morning paper when Water-rat burst into his room.

"Why, bless me!" he boomed. "An Unexpected Visitor, though not, I trust, a Dangerous One. You're too late for breakfast, my friend, but ring that hare-bell and call for red wine."

"Never mind about wine, Toad!" cried Water-rat. "Stir yourself. Danger is coming up the river. Escaped otter hounds."

Toad opened wide his great lamp-like eyes. Then he lowered his lids again.

"I have no fear, my dear Water-rat, of wild dogs," said he calmly. "They would not want to eat me, since there is no sweet taste in my warty, bumpy skin."

He took up his newspaper once more. "In any case, I am too proud, and too old, to run away. And," he added, turning a sheet of the newspaper, "I have a good many bottles of my famous Venom, ready for You Know Who."

"This won't do, Toad," said Water-rat severely. "Not only is the whole river bank in peril, but perhaps the hounds will turn inland and hunt other creatures. Hare, maybe. Or Grey Rabbit!"

Toad sat bolt upright. "Little Grey Rabbit," he muttered, reaching for his bell.

He got out of bed as quickly as his old bones would allow, nearly knocking over his breakfast tray as he did so.

Within minutes Toad had sent off several young frogs to spread the alarm in the surrounding countryside –

the brightest and the quickest of them charged with going straightway to the home of Squirrel, Hare and Grey Rabbit.

As Water-rat splashed back towards his boat, Old Toad's housekeeper caught him up, gasping for breath, and thrust two dark-coloured bottles into his arms. "Some of Toad's Venom," cried Water-rat in triumph.

"Many thanks!" he shouted as he pulled at the 'Saucy Nancy's' oars.

A little later Water-rat reached the jetty of his sister's house. His sister appeared, holding her arms out to greet him, but before she could say a word, even to observe how muddy he was, Water-rat had pulled her into his boat.

"You've splashed my clean blue dress!" his sister complained. "And crumpled my frilly collar." She seemed most put out.

"Hush!" hissed Water-rat sending his boat skimming over the water. Wild dogs are coming! Listen!"

In the distance, but getting nearer, came the sound of hounds baying. Water-rat's sister began to cry with fear.

"We'll never get away if we stay on the river," said Water-rat grimly.

"There's Kingfisher Creek," his sister sobbed. "Round the next bend of the river. But hurry!"

The terrible noise of the hounds, hungry for blood, came nearer and nearer.

At last the 'Saucy Nancy' turned into the narrow waters of Kingfisher Creek. Panting with exhaustion, Water-rat tied his boat to the roots of a tree and, holding his sister's hand, scrambled into the thick foliage at the creek's edge.

Peeping down the creek they saw the otter hounds sniffing along the river bank, twisting and turning as they sought their prey.

Water-rat put his paw over his sister's eyes. "Outrageous!" he whispered. "Why should they come here, terrifying the creatures of the river bank. What harm have we ever done them?"

At his side, his sister shed great silent tears as the noise of the hounds faded away.

Much later when all was quiet and safe, Water-rat took his sister home, and then rowed downriver.

Green dragonflies darted over his head, and the kingfisher flashed by like a swift blue arrow.

As the 'Saucy Nancy' slipped through the water, the swallows swooped over Water-rat's head. "Well done, Ratty!" they twittered. "You've saved the day!"

The otter family were outside their house when Water-rat passed by. "Glad to see you safe and sound," he called. "Oh thank you for your warning, my dear friend," shouted Mr Otter, and the young otter squeaked, "You're my hero!"

Water-rat blushed. "A hero!" said he to himself. He shook his head. "A fine hero, hiding away and trembling with fear." He sighed. "But at least none of us was hurt."

Then he pulled hard on the scarlet oars, and brought the 'Saucy Nancy' home as the sun began to dip in the western sky.

The Wandering Hedgehog
Settles Down

One day Brush, the Wandering Hedgehog, was sitting on a stool outside a hollow oak tree. He had recently returned from his travels and had tossed his old blanket and a few belongings into the hollow tree. "I need a rest, I do," he said to himself. "I'm that tired from my journeyings to Canada and the North Pole and suchlike places."

He had hung a piece of sacking across the hole in the tree to serve as a door. He had slept for three weeks. Some nights, when the wind blew, he had shivered on his bed of dried leaves and clutched his blanket round his shoulders.

But now it was a warm Spring day. The primroses were showing their yellow heads among the grass, and from nearby fields he could hear the new born lambs bleating to their mothers.

Suddenly he felt lonely. He could hardly remember his own mother, and he spent so much time tramping down strange lanes and by-ways that he never seemed to get to know anybody for very long.

Of course, there was Grey Rabbit. The last time he had been hereabouts, she had made him his coat of many colours. Hare and Squirrel had helped her, and many creatures had given little scraps of silk and wool, linen and calico, lichens and leaves. The Wandering Hedgehog stroked the front of the beautiful coat. It was a little grubby now from much wearing. "It's like a rainbow," said he. "Only once did I see a coat nearly as fine. When I was in China, long ago, the Emperor had a coat almost as good as this one."

He stood up. "I'll go a-visiting," he muttered. "My nephew Fuzzypeg lives yonder. I'll tell him about the far away places and people I've seed on my travels. He's a scholar, he is, and will understand."

But Fuzzypeg and his family weren't at home when the Wandering Hedgehog knocked on their door. So he walked on to Fuzzypeg's cousins, the twins Bill and Tim, who lived in a cottage in the larch wood.

What a happy scene he found. Bill and Tim, in their bright red smocks, were squeaking with delight as their father trundled them about in his wheelbarrow. Mrs Hedgehog was hanging up newly washed clothes on the line, and from the open door came the smell of freshly baked bread.

Soon the twins were sitting, their eyes open wide, listening to their Uncle Brush's tales. He told them of the snow mushrooms he had eaten in the freezing wastes of the North Pole. "And in Africky," he went on, "I ate sun-toasted mushrooms that growed in the desert. I was never short of a bite to eat there."

"He's an old romancer, your brother," said Mrs Hedgehog to her husband, shaking her head and laughing. But she went into the kitchen and cooked a whole panful of English mushrooms sprinkled with pepper and salt.

The Wandering Hedgehog smacked his lips at the feast, then wiped his greasy paws on his ragged trousers.

"Well, I'd best be getting home," said he. He looked round the cosy kitchen, at the sparkling saucepans and the blue and white curtains, and at the rush mats on the red-tiled floor. "Not that mine's much of a home," he said, sadly.

The Wandering Hedgehog spent the next few days dozing on his bed of dried leaves and feeling sorry for himself.

Then a visitor came, hallooing through his doorway and waking him up.

It was another wanderer, an old hedgehog called Snuffle. He had travelled even further, and had lived even harder than Brush.

The two travellers sat puffing the dried meadow-sweet in their pipes, and sipping from a pair of old, chipped mugs. "It's a rare drop of tay, is this," said Snuffle contentedly. "Thank'ee, my old friend."

"But," he went on, "I've tasted rarer herbs than these in the steamy jungles of South Americky, and the secret spices of India take a bit o' beating."

Brush nodded. "I did once get as far as India," he said. "But I've never been to South Americky. I should love to see Peru and the woolly llamas in the Andes mountains."

"Come with me!" urged his friend. "I've a fancy to get aboard a ship and travel to Brazil or Peru or some such place."

The Wandering Hedgehog's eyes sparkled. But then

153

he shook his head. "No, old friend, it's very kind of you, but I've done with travelling; for a bit anyway. I'm thinking of staying put. I'm going to settle down."

Snuffle stood up, his mouth wide open. "Going to settle down?" he cried in amazement. "Why, what's the use in that? You'll get stuck in a rut, you will. You'll be as dull as ditch-water. You'll . . ."

But words failed him, and he stood there muttering to himself and scratching his spiky head. At last he picked up his bundle of belongings and shuffled off.

As Brush watched him disappear he remembered the words of the song he used to sing on his travels, and before he was given his coat of many colours:

I haven't got a coat, and I haven't got a shoe,
I haven't got a penny, and I haven't got a sou.
I don't care a jot, I've got my cooking-pot,
And the whole wide world is mine to wander
    through.

Well, things were different now. He already had his beautiful coat, and although he still had no need for shoes or money, he no longer wanted to wander weary miles down unknown lanes.

So the Wandering Hedgehog began to settle down. He set to work on tidying up his home in the hollow oak. He hung a curtain in place of the piece of sacking, and widened the doorway. Then he put another window in the trunk to let in more light. He threw out the dried leaves and stuffed a mattress with clean straw. Hare gave him a sturdy spare chair with a straight back, and Water-rat cut him a bundle of rushes to use as a carpet. Grey Rabbit made curtains for his windows, and Squirrel knitted a green tea cosy for the teapot. Even Wise Owl dropped a book on his door-step one night. It was an atlas of the world, and whenever the Wandering Hedgehog felt his old urge to travel afar, he turned the pages and peered at the maps instead, imagining that he was across the seas among strange beasts and birds and people.

He had no need of money, even though Moldy Warp the mole made him a present of a battered coin he had dug out of the ground near the old Roman road. There was the head of some long dead monarch

upon it, and the Wandering Hedgehog, who polished the coin and hung it on his wall as an ornament, swore that it was a picture of his old friend, the Emperor of China.

At any rate, the money was never spent. Every morning Milkman Hedgehog brought him milk still warm from the cow, and the Speckledy Hen regularly appeared to give him a new laid egg and to admire his clean and cheery little home. Grey Rabbit and Mrs Hedgehog left him cakes and pies.

In return, the Wandering Hedgehog made his friends all manner of things: flutes from elder stems, bracelets and bangles from flowers and grasses, scarves from gossamer and purses from bats' wing.

But what they liked best was when he told them tales of his adventures. They would gather round his cherry-wood fire, and share the good broth that he cooked from all the wild things of the hedgerows. And when they were comfortable and well fed the Wandering Hedgehog would begin his yarns.

Then they would be carried far away on the wings of the wind, or imagine themselves on great ships or clinging onto dog-sleds at the North Pole. They would forget their little troubles and their aches and pains, so enchanted were they. Sometimes they would even forget where they were and would have to shake themselves out of their dreams when the stories came to an end.

As for the Wandering Hedgehog, he does seem to have settled down. But who knows? One day he may get tired of staying in one place, comfortable though it is. Then he will pack up a few belongings, say goodbye to his friends, and quietly slip away, singing under the stars.